–The–
Mayflower
Secret

Trailblazer Books

Gladys Aylward • *Flight of the Fugitives*
Mary McLeod Bethune • *Defeat of the Ghost Riders*
William & Catherine Booth • *Kidnapped by River Rats*
Governor William Bradford • *The Mayflower Secret*
John Bunyan • *Traitor in the Tower*
Amy Carmichael • *The Hidden Jewel*
Peter Cartwright • *Abandoned on the Wild Frontier*
Elizabeth Fry • *The Thieves of Tyburn Square*
Jonathan & Rosalind Goforth • *Mask of the Wolf Boy*
Sheldon Jackson • *The Gold Miners' Rescue*
Adoniram & Ann Judson • *Imprisoned in the Golden City*
Festo Kivengere • *Assassins in the Cathedral*
David Livingstone • *Escape from the Slave Traders*
Martin Luther • *Spy for the Night Riders*
Dwight L. Moody • *Danger on the Flying Trapeze*
Samuel Morris • *Quest for the Lost Prince*
George Müller • *The Bandit of Ashley Downs*
John Newton • *The Runaway's Revenge*
Florence Nightingale • *The Drummer Boy's Battle*
Nate Saint • *The Fate of the Yellow Woodbee*
Menno Simons • *The Betrayer's Fortune*
Mary Slessor • *Trial by Poison*
Hudson Taylor • *Shanghaied to China*
Harriet Tubman • *Listen for the Whippoorwill*
William Tyndale • *The Queen's Smuggler*
John Wesley • *The Chimney Sweep's Ransom*
Marcus & Narcissa Whitman • *Attack in the Rye Grass*
David Zeisberger • *The Warrior's Challenge*

Also by Dave and Neta Jackson

*Hero Tales: A Family Treasury of True Stories
From the Lives of Christian Heroes* (Volumes I, II, & III)

–The–
Mayflower
Secret

Dave & Neta Jackson

Story illustrations by
Julian Jackson

BETHANY HOUSE PUBLISHERS
MINNEAPOLIS, MINNESOTA 55438

Published by Bethany House Publishers
A Ministry of Bethany Fellowship International
11400 Hampshire Avenue South
Minneapolis, Minnesota 55438
www.bethanyhouse.com

Printed in the United States of America by
Bethany Press International, Minneapolis, Minnesota 55438

Library of Congress Cataloging-in-Publication Data

Jackson, Dave
    The Mayflower secret / Dave and Neta Jackson.
       p.   cm. — (Trailblazer books)
    Summary: Teenage Elizabeth Tilley, one of the colonists landing at New Plymouth on the Mayflower, sees her parents die from illness and wonders if God is punishing her for the terrible secret she carries.
    ISBN 0–7642–2010–1 (pbk.)
    1. Tilley, Elizabeth, 1607–1687 or 8—Juvenile fiction. 2. Pilgrims (New Plymouth Colony)—Juvenile fiction. [1. Tilley, Elizabeth, 1607–1687 or 8—Fiction. 2. Pilgrims (New Plymouth Colony)—Fiction.
3. Massachusetts—History—New Plymouth, 1620–1691—Fiction.
4. Orphans—Fiction. 5. Christian life—Fiction.]
    I. Jackson, Neta. II. Title. III. Series: Jackson, Dave. Trailblazer books.
PZ7.J132418May   1998
[Fic]—dc21   97–45439
                                               CIP
                                             AC

Elizabeth Tilley, left an orphan at the age of fourteen when her parents died the first winter at Plymouth, married John Howland in 1623 when she was barely sixteen. Our story has the marriage take place in the summer; however, a belated source we found on the Howland family marks the date in the spring of that year.

While the events surrounding the disappearance and presumed drowning of Dorothy Bradford are true, Elizabeth Tilley's involvement and the subsequent secret are entirely fictional.

It is known who the principal persons assigned to the first seven houses at Plymouth Plantation were, but it is not as clearly documented how the rest of the families, single men, and orphans were distributed among these "households."

The name of Hobomok's wife is fictional; all other names refer to real persons.

The colonists at Plymouth were not called "Pilgrims" until the mid-1800s. They referred to themselves as "Brethren."

The dates referred to in this story are according to the Julian calendar, which the Plymouth colonists used. To get the equivalent date according to our modern calendar (the Gregorian), add ten days.

DAVE AND NETA JACKSON are a husband/wife writing team who have authored and coauthored many books on marriage and family, the church, and relationships, including the books accompanying the Secret Adventures video series, the Pet Parables series, the Caring Parent series, and the newly released *Hero Tales,* volumes I and II.

The Jacksons have two married children: Julian, the illustrator for TRAILBLAZER BOOKS, and Rachel, who has recently blessed them with a granddaughter, Havah Noelle. Dave and Neta make their home in Evanston, Illinois, where they are active members of Reba Place Church.

CONTENTS

Chapter 1

Saints and Strangers

ELIZABETH TILLEY STARED in dismay as more men, women, and children cautiously made their way down the narrow ship's ladder. As if the *Mayflower* wasn't crowded enough already! "Move along! Move along!" rasped a sailor's voice above on the main deck as passengers from the leaking *Speedwell* were herded below to the tween deck of its sister ship.

"I'll not go, I tell thee, husband!" A shrill voice from among the ninety passengers already crammed in the tween deck rose above the babble of voices. " 'Twas crowded before; now 'tis like rotten apples crushed in a cider press. Thou canst go to the New World with these fanatical Separatists if thee wants to, but I am getting off this miserable ship."

"Thou wilt do no such thing!" snapped a man.

Thirteen-year-old Elizabeth rolled her eyes, which were green as seawater. It was those Billingtons, quarreling again. For all she cared, they could get off and give the rest of them more room. She, too, was tired of living on board the crowded ship. And they hadn't even left England yet!

The crew and passengers of the *Mayflower* and the *Speedwell* had hoped to leave England in June that year of 1620, but problems in getting supplies and endless arguments over the contract with the Merchant Adventurers, who were financing the voyage, had delayed their departure. In August the two ships had gotten underway, but twice now they'd had to turn back because the *Speedwell*, the smaller of the two ships, had begun leaking. Finally, abandoned as unseaworthy, the *Speedwell's* passengers were being transferred to the larger ship. Now it was September, and they were still anchored in Plymouth Bay, England!

Families—the lucky ones—had been assigned "cabins," each consisting of a sleeping platform about three feet by five feet built against the hull of the ship, separated on each end from other "cabins" by wooden dividers. Hanging a piece of cloth between the dividers provided a little privacy—but, in general, men, women, and children were jumbled together like stew in a pot. Other families, and most of the single men and servants, had to sleep on the deck wherever a few feet of space could be found. And now they had to share even *that* with the newcomers.

Elizabeth was glad some of the passengers had changed their minds about going on this voyage. Weed out the weak-hearted ones now. But there would be no turning back for the Tilley family. She had overheard her father and Uncle Edward talking on the other side of the curtain last night as she and her mother huddled under their blankets. . . .

"What's there to go back to, Edward?" her father said quietly. "The silk-weaving business was just barely gettin' us by. We did the right thing sellin' off the business and gettin' out when we did."

"Thy gambling debts didn't help any," her mother grumbled. Elizabeth sucked in her breath. Her father's gambling was a sore subject. At first the cock fights and boxing matches at the local tavern had only been a bit of fun with the other men every so often. Then, feeling lucky, her father began betting more money. When he lost, he bet more, hoping to pay off the debts that were piling up. That's when the nagging and yelling began at home.

"Guard thy tongue, wife, and go to sleep," said her father. "What's done is done. Make the best of it."

The Tilley brothers lowered their voices even further, and Elizabeth had to strain to hear. "Land—that's where the real money is, brother," her father went on. "To own land, to be your own master—isn't that every Englishman's dream? But is there any land to be had in England? Nay! But in the New World, now, that's different."

"Perchance, John," said her uncle. "But what dost thou make of these Puritan Separatists? First they run away to Holland; now it's off to the New World with talk of 'freedom of religion.' Why do they want to have a separate church anyway? Think they're too good for the Church of England, that's what. Make too much of religion, if thou asks me. The whole lot of them, always singing and praying—even when it's not the Sabbath! Humph. Maybe we're asking for trouble throwing in our lot with them. That Brewster fellow, for instance. A printer by trade, but 'Elder Brewster' they call him. Hasn't dared to show his face above deck as long as we're in England—got a price on his head for some fool tract he printed, I hear."

Elizabeth heard her father chuckle. "Perchance, brother. But the feud between King James and these Puritan Separatists works to our advantage. They're not welcome in England, so now they're determined to set up a colony in the New World, where they can worship as they please. But they can't do it alone— which is why Weston and his Adventurers recruited the likes of us! It's our chance to make our fortune!"

There was a long silence. Then Elizabeth's uncle spoke again. "Sometimes I wonder, brother . . . what good will it be to make a fortune? When we are gone, the Tilley name goes to the grave with us."

Elizabeth winced under her blanket. She was the youngest of five children born to John and Joan Tilley. The first two had died of fevers—a wee boy *and later a wee girl. The next two sisters survived, but they had been married off as quickly as possible while there was still some money to give them a small dowry. Now Elizabeth was the only one yet at home. She supposed her father loved her well enough, but she knew it was a disappointment to him that he had no son to carry on the family name. And Uncle Edward and Auntie Ann were childless except for her aunt's orphan cousins she'd taken in to raise—young Henry Samson, who was ten, and eight-year-old Humility Cooper. But she'd show her father. He wouldn't regret taking her to the New World. Son or no, she'd help him make his fortune in the—*

"Oh, Cousin Eliza!" Humility's childish voice broke into Elizabeth's thoughts. "Come and see the doggies!" The little girl's brown eyes were dancing under her *coif,* a white cap that was used to tuck up the hair of all women and girls in seventeenth century England. Elizabeth's own mop of red curls was tucked up into her coif, though the unruly curls had a way of escaping from under the cap no matter how many pins she used. "Truly!" Humility bubbled on. "One is almost as big as a pony! And a dear, sweet spaniel, white with brown spots."

"Do come on," hissed Henry in a whisper, "before Auntie Ann gives us more tasks to do."

Elizabeth longed to escape the jostling bodies and stifling air in the tween deck as everyone made room for the new passengers. Maybe she could find Mary Chilton, the one friend she'd made so far on board ship. But one look at her mother's flustered face and she shook her head. "Perchance later, Humility. We must make up the bedding for Mam and Auntie Ann. Henry, help me move these coals before someone tips the brazier over and we set the whole ship on fire."

The small iron brazier sitting in its box of sand served as the only means to cook their food on board ship. As the cousins carefully moved the smoking pan of coals out of the way of clomping shoes and long skirts pushing past, Elizabeth heard a timid voice say, "Beg pardon, Goodwife."

Looking up, Elizabeth saw a slender young woman wearing a maroon-colored cape, her dark hair peeking from under her coif, and looking quite lost. Elizabeth had seen her many times on the docks at Southampton and Dartmouth as the passengers from the two sister ships had mingled and waited, waited and mingled. She was the wife of one of the Separatist leaders, though she hardly looked older than a girl herself. Now she was trying to speak to Elizabeth's mother, who was rearranging bundles under the sleeping platform. "Could I ... I mean, wouldst thou mind—" The woman stopped helplessly.

"Eh?" Joan Tilley straightened up, all a-fluster. "Oh! Good day, Mistress Bradford. Would thou be looking for a place to set thy bundles, then?" The young woman nodded gratefully. Joan Tilley cocked a curious eyebrow. "And where is thy husband, Mistress Bradford? Tsk, tsk—leaving thee to settle aboard all by thyself. The way of men, aye?"

The young Mistress Bradford managed a pale

14

smile. "He's above, talking to Master Weston—"

"Marry! Still arguing about the contract!" said Joan Tilley. "Well, I hope he gives that weasel a piece of his mind. Never met the like! Says one thing today, something different tomorrow. Well, now," she said, looking around, "surely we can find thee a wee spot of room to put thy bundles."

Grabbing Humility and Henry by the hand, Elizabeth scrambled up the ladder to the main deck. *Huh!* she thought. *That woman looks like a pampered china doll. Taking her on a dangerous sea voyage is like turning a butterfly loose in a thunderstorm.*

An argument was in full swing on the main deck. "These terms are outrageous, Master Weston!" an older man in a white lace collar, dark green doublet, and well-cut breeches said. Elizabeth had heard the Separatists call him Master Carver—a wealthy man by all appearances. The Carvers had no children but several servants. "Not even two days to work for ourselves?" Carver fumed. "And *all* to be divided— even houses and fields—at the end of seven years?"

The man named Weston shrugged. A twist of gold-colored cloth ringed his felt hat, and gold garters held up yellow stockings. Elizabeth recognized him as the man who had recruited her father for this voyage to the New World. As Elizabeth and her cousins squeezed past, she heard the man say firmly, "Those are my terms, gentlemen. My stockholders must gain interest on their investment."

"*Interest!*" exploded Carver. "This is robbery!"

A calm voice intervened. "Thy people are investing mere money, Master Weston; our people are investing their very lives in this undertaking. Who knows what awaits us in the new land?" The speaker was nearly six feet tall, maybe thirty years old, a handsome man, bearded, with a firm jaw and serious gray eyes. Master Bradford, Elizabeth thought, the china doll's husband. "But," Bradford continued, "we have no choice but to accept thy terms. We must sail with the tide. Good day, Weston."

Weston merely shrugged and with a sly smile climbed over the side of the ship to the longboat below, which would take him back to the dock.

"Come on, Eliza!" wailed Humilty, pulling on Elizabeth's sleeve.

Elizabeth allowed herself to be dragged across the narrow deck to the main mast, where a young man with a shock of sandy brown hair—she guessed him to be twenty-one or twenty-two—was holding two dogs, a huge mastiff and an English spaniel, by their leather leashes. Young Henry was tussling with the spaniel and getting his face licked in return.

"Thy dogs?" Elizabeth asked politely.

The young man's face turned red. "Nay, miss. They belong to John Goodman. He asked me to hold them while he said good-bye to his new wife." He seemed to be staring at Elizabeth's freckled face.

Her manner cooled. "And thou art—?"

"John Howland, miss. Bond servant to Master Carver. Like a father he's been." The color in the young man's face deepened, as if he had blurted out too much.

"Oh, Eliza!" Humility giggled as she wrapped her

arms around the huge, brindle-colored mastiff. "This one's name is Bear!" Elizabeth turned away, trying to look bored. She wished Humility wouldn't call her Eliza. The young man was just a servant, after all.

"*There* you are!" Mary Chilton, who was fifteen, pulled Elizabeth around to the other side of the main mast, which stood like a massive tree trunk in the middle of a forest of ship's rigging and furled sails. "Must thou always be tied to those silly cousins of thine?" she asked in mock horror. "And gossiping with the servants, too!"

Elizabeth started to protest, but Mary babbled right on. "We're sailing today in truth. Look!" She pointed to a short, pompous man with a dark reddish beard, wearing a helmet and sword, who was helping a weeping young woman climb down the rope ladder into a longboat below. "I heard the ship's master tell Captain Standish to get all visitors off the ship—the tide is about to turn."

" 'Captain Shrimp,' thou means," Elizabeth smirked.

Mary's eyes widened. "Nay! Who calls him that? Not his sweet wife, Rose!" But Mary, too, started to laugh behind her hand.

"The sailors. They were making fun of him when he was drilling the men on deck." Everyone knew that the dashing Captain Myles Standish had been recruited by Master Weston to form a militia to protect the new colony. Elizabeth grinned impishly.

The girls' giggles were interrupted as the first mate began shouting orders from the quarterdeck. Suddenly, the top decks became an anthill of activity as sailors started climbing the rigging to loosen the sails and others began turning the windlass, which pulled up the anchor. "Oot the way, lassies!" beckoned Captain Standish, rattling the sword at his side impatiently. His Scottish accent was crisp and demanding. "Get the children and thyselves below!"

They sailed with the tide. Twenty passengers from the *Speedwell* had decided to stay behind, leaving 102 on board the *Mayflower*. Forty-one were Puritan Separatists, or "Brethren," as they called themselves. The majority were ordinary Englishmen, loyal subjects of King James and members by birth of the Church of England. They would have been surprised to know that the Brethren referred to them kindly as "Strangers." Not so kindly, some of the sailors sneered at the Separatists and called them "Saints" as if it were a dirty word.

Once the *Mayflower* had cleared Plymouth Harbor, the ship caught a fair breeze under full sail. Cleared earlier from the deck out of the sailors' way, both Saints and Strangers now began to drift back to the main deck for one last look at their homeland. The sun was sinking before the ship's bow in the west, reflecting off the windows of Plymouth behind them like fiery rubies in an emerald necklace.

Escaping her young foster cousins, Elizabeth climbed up the ladder to the quarterdeck and made her way toward the rear of the ship for a better view.

She felt a sudden sadness at leaving all she'd ever
known. She wasn't close to her married sisters . . .

but would she ever see them again? At the same time she felt a flutter of excitement. Father was right. There was nothing left for them here in England. But a new land, a new home—there they could get a new start. There she would discover her place.

Elizabeth's thoughts were interrupted by two voices behind her on the other side of the mizzen-mast. "Oh, William, did we have to leave him behind?" a woman's voice moaned as if in pain.

"Dority, Dority," soothed a man's voice. "Don't do this to thyself. Thou knows why we left him with Pastor Robinson. A sea voyage late in the year, an untamed land—thou knows the dangers. But as soon as we build homes in the wilderness and find a way to keep ourselves alive, we will send for wee John."

Elizabeth could hear muffled sobs. She inched farther along the rail, trying to see who was crying.

"But," the woman sniffed, "the Whites brought their son, Resolved, and he's five, same as John. Wrestling Brewster is only four. And wee Mary Allerton is a mere sucking child! Oh, William, if other parents could bring their children—" The sobs grew louder.

"Dority, stop. Thou wilt make thyself sick. We made the best decision we knew how. Others also left children behind. Come, come, now, dry thy tears. God will give us the strength to endure." The couple slowly moved out of the shadows and made their way toward the ladder. The woman was almost hidden by her husband's arm and long cape wrapped around her. But Elizabeth recognized them immediately.

Dorothy, the china doll wife, and William Bradford.

Chapter 2

Overboard!

ELIZABETH OPENED HER EYES, and even in the semi-darkness of the tween deck, she knew it was daylight. But something was different this morning. Then she realized that for the first time in three days she didn't feel seasick.

She heard singing up on the main deck. The Separatist Brethren were having their morning prayers and psalm singing. Moving quietly so as not to awaken her sleeping mother, Elizabeth pushed aside the curtain of their cabin and crawled off the straw mattress. She was still wearing the same clothes she'd been wearing when they left England.

Oh, what she wouldn't give for a good wash! But, Saints or no Saints, she needed some fresh air.

Tucking stray red curls back under her coif, Elizabeth made her way unsteadily toward the ladder. Some of the non-Separatist passengers were still sleeping, but Mistress Hopkins, stirring a pot of bean porridge simmering on a brazier, murmured "Good day" as she passed. Three young children lay sprawled on the family bed, but Elizabeth noticed with interest that Mistress Hopkins was surely going to have another child—and right soon. Two other women were also large with child: Susanna White and Mary Allerton, both Separatists. She wondered which of the three women would give birth first.

Peeking through the hatch at the top of the ladder, Elizabeth could see the little knot of Separatists on the quarterdeck. The huge sails filled the sky like proud wings. But between the sails she was grateful to see that the sky was still crystal blue. Everyone knew it was late in the year to sail across the Atlantic. But blue skies and a steady wind helped calm the nervous passengers. Still, it took a while for Elizabeth to get used to the constant motion of the *Mayflower* plowing through the ocean swells. She wasn't sure which was worse: throwing up in a common bucket or having to lug the bucket to an open porthole to heave its contents overboard.

"Goot day, miss." A strong hand helped her up the ladder. Captain Myles Standish, puffing out his red doublet like a bantam rooster, tipped his hat as he helped her to the ship's rail. *He's probably never been seasick in his life*, Elizabeth thought.

Gratefully, the girl filled her lungs with the clean, cool sea air. A few minutes later Mary Chilton, still looking a little green, joined her at the rail. "Perchance the worst of it's over," Elizabeth soothed her friend. "Father said that Master Jones is taking the direct route across the Atlantic to the New World because of the late season. If the weather holds—"

"Out ta way. Out ta way," growled a raspy voice behind them. A hard-faced sailor in a knit cap was trying to swab down the main deck. "Huh! Bad 'nough trippin' over passengers on a cargo ship 'thout havin' ta listen to the religious fanatics up there yowlin' like cats on a fence. Huh!" His mop splashed Elizabeth's feet for emphasis. "Why can't they do their singin' in church like reg'lar folk?"

Elizabeth made a face. The rough language of the sailors was much more unpleasant than the plain, sweet singing of the Separatists, strange as they were.

The worshipers on the quarterdeck were beginning to disband when suddenly a deep voice boomed, "All hands on deck! Prepare to come about!" A bell rang and sailors set to work. Elizabeth and Mary scurried to get out of the way, but some of the male passengers already on deck leaped to give a hand to a maneuver that was becoming familiar.

Since the wind was coming out of the west, Master Jones, the ship's captain, had to tack back, zigzag fashion, to make any headway. To "come about" or change direction, the helmsman swung the tiller hard, and the sailors and their helpers pulled hard on the ropes that readjusted the main sail.

Ducking into the open area beneath the quarter-deck, Elizabeth and Mary clung to the big winch used to hoist cargo onto the ship. The great sails flapped in protest as the ship creaked and swung around in its new direction. Then the sails caught the wind with a boom like a small cannon, and the ship seemed to leap over the swells.

Several other women and children had taken refuge under the quarterdeck. Mistress Bradford, her eyes large and skin pale, held little Resolved White protectively against her skirt. The little boy, whose name meant "resolved to follow the Lord," wore a long, homespun dress and white cap. His mother, Susanna White, smiled at her friend. "Resolved isn't going to fall overboard, Dorothy," she laughed gently. "Truly, he'll be all right. See, the ship has come about and is on course again." The woman patted her swelling stomach and sighed. "I just pray this one waits to arrive till we reach our new home."

Elizabeth caught Mary's eye and made a face. She liked babies all right. A lot better than half-grown pesky cousins. But it seemed a folly to leave England for a wild and unknown country just before a birthing.

The Separatist women were joined by another mother and child. "Oh! Here's Elizabeth Winslow and wee Ellen More," said Susanna. Resolved let go of Dorothy Bradford's skirts and clapped his hands.

"Methinks Resolved and Ellen want to play," laughed the newcomer.

"Yes, but—oof! I must get off my feet," wheezed

Susanna. "Dorothy, couldst thou tend Resolved? Just hold on to his strings." The mother-to-be carefully made her way toward the hatch that led below.

Elizabeth wondered if Mistress White really had to get off her feet, or if she just felt sorry for Dorothy Bradford, whose own child had been left behind. She felt a twinge of irritation. Everybody seemed to feel sorry for Mistress Bradford. Well, not Elizabeth. Hadn't everyone left somebody behind? The woman was just going to have to lift her chin up.

Mary leaned close to Elizabeth's ear. "See wee Ellen More there with Mistress Winslow?" she whispered. "Didst thou notice that three different families among the Separatists are caring for children named More? The Carvers have the older boy, and the Brewsters have taken the other two boys as companions for their sons, Love and Wrestling—"

Elizabeth giggled. " 'Love' and 'Wrestling'! What strange names these Separatists give their children!"

"Something dreadful must have happened to their parents," Mary whispered dramatically.

"Or maybe Goodman More ran off with a barmaid and Goody More died of a broken heart." The girls tried to stifle their giggles.

Boredom was a constant companion on board ship. As the two girls entertained themselves gossiping about the other passengers, the *Mayflower* coaxed the light, westerly winds into its sails as if trying to hold on to the fair weather and good fortune.

The fair weather did not hold. In late September slate gray skies unleashed strong winds, and the ship battled hard to make progress through the high seas. Going up on the main deck for fresh air now meant clinging hard to the rigging and getting thoroughly damp from the constant spray of the waves.

It was no longer possible to cook with the braziers. Wrinkling her nose in disgust, Elizabeth cut away green mold from their cheese ration before giving Humility and Henry their portion, along with salted beef and hardtack, a tough biscuit. This cold meal was washed down with "small beer," a weak beer that was safer than the water in the ship's hold, which had turned scummy and brown in its barrels.

Then one night Elizabeth was shaken awake by her mother. "Take the three Hopkins children into our bed," said Joan Tilley. "Quickly now."

Elizabeth could hear moans and gasps from the other side of the crowded tween deck. Three children stood wide-eyed and silent beside the Hopkins' cabin, where Stephen Hopkins, a wool merchant, comforted his laboring wife. Picking up little Damaris Hopkins in one arm, Elizabeth quickly herded the other two—Giles and Constance—back to the Tilley bed.

"Thy mother is going to be fine," Elizabeth soothed, rocking Damaris, who was holding tightly to her poppet, a homemade doll. "And soon thou will have a new wee brother or sister."

John Tilley, sleeping while half sitting against the cabin partition, mumbled in his sleep. Elizabeth put a finger to her lips. "Let's sing a song," she

whispered. As the ship rolled and pitched through-
out the black night, Elizabeth quietly sang all the

nursery rhymes she could remember until the three children fell asleep. She, too, dozed off but was awakened again, this time by a new sound.

A baby's cry.

Much later, her mother finally crawled into the crowded bed, leaning wearily against the partition.

"Boy or girl?" Elizabeth whispered eagerly.

"Boy," murmured Joan Tilley. "Alive and well."

"Name?" the girl asked impatiently.

There was a smile in her mother's voice. "Oceanus."

Thirty days passed, then forty. Storms lashed the ship day and night. By now it was obvious not only to the crew, but to the passengers, that the "shortcut" across the Atlantic was taking much longer than everyone had hoped. Tempers were short and tension increased between the frightened passengers and the disgruntled sailors. Master Jones tried to keep his crew in check, but several sailors openly cursed the Separatists when they tried to hold daily prayers. A few of the passengers—especially Dorothy Bradford—became seriously ill with the poor food and constant seasickness. The ship's master took pity on Bradford's wife and had her moved to his own cabin, away from the stifling smells and crowded conditions of the tween deck.

High seas made it next to impossible to do anything except hold on and pray. There was no more playing among the children, as parents held on to their little ones to keep them from being tossed about like fragile eggs. The psalm singing and praying increased. Elizabeth, huddled day after day with Humility and Henry in their cabin, found it strangely comforting. Back in England, her parents had gone to church occasionally—for baptisms and weddings and Christmas. It was just something that everyone did. But these Separatists talked to God as if He was in charge of even everyday things.

CRAAAAACK!

Elizabeth sat bolt upright in bed. What was that? She could tell from the pitch of the ship and the roaring of the wind that a fierce storm was raging outside. Suddenly, everything was mass confusion.

"A beam has broken!" . . . "Water is pouring in!" . . . "Get the captain!" . . . "All men on deck!"

Small children were wailing and men were shouting. Frightened, Elizabeth peeked from behind the curtain. Each time the ship rolled, water came pouring in from the main deck above. Soon everything and everyone below decks was sopping wet.

The Tilley brothers soon came back with news. "The big beam under the main deck is cracked!" cried Elizabeth's father. "The sailors want to turn back to England and go with the wind. Too much stress on the ship to continue battling these westerly gales—"

"But Carver and Bradford said they have a giant screw in the hold," Edward Tilley broke in. "The Separatists brought it to lift timbers and build homes in the wilderness. Bradford is certain we can shore up the beam and make it secure."

Elizabeth could hear prayers all around her. Even some of the non-Separatists were praying aloud. Sailors and passengers alike worked feverishly to haul up the large screw from the hold in the bottom of the ship and get it in place. It took many men to brace the screw in the right position and then turn the screw beneath the cracked beam. *Screeeech! Screeeech! Screeeech!* The sound of the turning screw was almost lost in the battering of the storm outside.

But it worked. The beam held. Cheers rose, and not one sailor grumbled when the Separatists kneeled down and offered prayers of thanksgiving.

Without the sun, however, the passengers couldn't get dry, and many developed colds and coughs. Elizabeth forced herself to eat, but she gagged on the wormy biscuits and could hardly swallow the stiff, salty beef. Still, the *Mayflower* struggled on, tacking its way back and forth across the westerly winds. But now when the cry "All hands on deck! Prepare to come about!" went up, only the youngest men among the passengers crawled up the ladder to help turn the ship in the heavy seas.

Then one day, when Master Jones had rolled up the sails to ride out the winds, came the dread cry, "Man overboard! Man overboard!"

Instantly, everyone froze. Who was it? Wives looked at one another. Children were silent, too scared to cry. Even the dogs sensed something was wrong and whimpered. Mary Chilton crawled over the lurching deck to the Tilley cabin, and the two girls clutched each other. *Who was it?*

A shout said, "It's young Howland!"

Elizabeth stared at Mary guiltily. The girls had often teased the young man. It was so much fun making him blush! After all, he was just a servant— jolly fair game for their jokes and pranks. That was their excuse, anyway. But God have mercy! What if—

The only sounds were the roaring winds and the groaning of the ship as the deep waves tossed it from side to side. Then—

"He caught a trailing halyard!" came the shout down the hatch. "They're pulling him in now with the boathook!"

The girls relaxed as they heard the shouts and cheers. Elizabeth grinned in relief at Mary, her guilty feelings dissolving like an icicle over a hot flame. "Perchance Master Carver thought his servant needed a bath!" she snickered. "Now he'll be the only man on board who doesn't smell like a barnyard."

Elizabeth was cold. Her damp clothes simply refused to dry. Fifty days at sea . . . or was it sixty? She'd lost count. She thought it was November. But what did it matter? They were probably lost and would never set foot on dry ground again.

She shut her eyes and pulled the wool blanket tighter around her shoulders. She was hungry, but if she had to eat one more strip of salted beef, she might scream. But, oh, what she wouldn't give for a steaming hot cup of tea, with cream from a cow . . .

and soft bread with fresh butter . . . or Mam's bean porridge bubbling over a hot fire.

"Thou must get up, miss," said a kindly man's voice. "Thou, too, Goodman Tilley. Get thy family up on deck and walk around. Thou must get thy blood moving. Come. The sun has broken through."

Elizabeth's eyes opened and focused. William Bradford was gently shaking her father awake. Then the Separatist leader moved on to the next family. "Master Mullins, get young Joseph and thy daughter, Priscilla, onto the deck. We must keep the blood moving. . . . Good day, Goodman Billington."

Grumbling but obedient, John Tilley prodded his wife and Elizabeth till they struggled up the ship's ladder to the main deck. A brisk, chill wind was blowing, but the storms had passed and the sun streaked through the broken clouds. Elizabeth forced her legs to walk from the open hatch to the main mast, then back. Then again to the main mast and back. Reluctantly, Elizabeth had to admit the exercise made her feel warmer, even up here in the wind.

"Land!" cried a voice up in the sails. "Land, ho!"

A shiver of disbelief shook Elizabeth's body. Could it really be . . . land? Sailors came running. Cries of hope rippled through the passengers. Those below came up on deck and peered into the horizon. Master Jones mounted the high poop deck with a telescope and looked a long time. Then he lowered the glass and turned to the anxious faces upturned toward him.

A smile broke on his weathered face. "Yes, it's land, by God's grace! Yonder is Cape Cod!"

Chapter 3

A Strange Disappearance

"WHAT DAY IS IT?" a hoarse voice yelled.

"November ninth," said the ship's master.

An astonished murmur rolled through the passengers clustered on deck. They had been at sea sixty-five days—twice as long as Columbus's voyage of discovery more than a century earlier.

But joy washed over the dirty, weary, sick travelers at the sight of land. Elizabeth and her friend Mary hugged each other. Humility and Henry hopped up and down. The dogs barked. Men clapped one another on the back. Many women wiped tears of relief from their raw, chapped faces. Even Mistress Hopkins and her new baby were helped up the ladder to the main deck to share the happy moment.

"Let us give thanks to God, who has delivered us safely to these shores," called out Elder Brewster, "and remember those among us who gave their lives on this journey." Two men had died from sickness on the long voyage—the crusty old sailor and one of the servants. But even the sailors held their tongues as the Separatists fell to their knees.

No sooner had the prayers ended than John Billington pushed his way toward Master Jones. "Didst thou say Cape Cod?"

"Aye."

"I thought our charter was for Virginia. Isn't that several hundred miles to the south?"

"Aye. But winter is almost upon us, good man. I would advise thee to set thyselves ashore and build shelter as quickly as possible."

"Master Jones speaks rightly," added William Bradford. "We must explore these shores for a fresh water supply and settle quickly."

"It's a goodly land," agreed Master Carver. "Look. Forests clear to the shoreline. Plenty of wood for fuel and building." The ship had sailed closer to the shore, and the thick carpet of trees hugging the water was visible to the naked eye.

Now many voices chimed in. "Put in to a safe harbor, Master Jones." ... "Supplies are low. We must find food soon!" ... "New England, Virginia—what difference does it make?"

All that day, the *Mayflower* crept south along the shore of the Cape, looking for a good harbor. Hungry for the sight of land, many of the passengers stayed on deck, even in the biting November winds. Elizabeth pulled her wool cape around her and stared at the rocky shores. How she longed to get off this crowded, miserable ship! But on shore there were no towns, no farms, no familiar English faces. What *was* out there? Wild animals? Strange native people? She shivered, only partly from the cold.

Making her way down the ladder to the tween deck out of the wind, Elizabeth saw John Billington talking with Stephen Hopkins, her father and Uncle Edward, and several other men.

"I tell thee," John Billington was saying, "the rules of our patent are only binding if we land in Virginia. If we land here, each man can do as he pleases."

"What dost thou mean, Billington?" said John Tilley. "Surely we need to stand by one another to survive the wilderness."

"Oh, aye. Neighbor to neighbor. But I, for one, am tired of being thrown scraps like a dog under the table. Each man for himself, I say."

Stephen Hopkins snorted appreciatively.

"But thou art talking anarchy!" said John Alden. Twenty-one and unmarried, Alden was tall and muscular. As a barrel maker, he had worked hard during the rough sea voyage to keep the barrels of flour, beer, salted meat, and other supplies watertight.

Elizabeth pressed her lips together and pushed past the men as they argued. That Billington. They hadn't even set foot on dry ground and he was stirring up trouble. A tremor of anxiety fluttered in her chest. Would everyone truly go their own way here in the new land? They had cut off all ties to England. The people on this ship were her only link to whatever her future held. They *had* to stay together.

Unable to find a safe harbor along the outside elbow of Cape Cod, the *Mayflower* turned around and headed north again, finally dropping anchor in the early hours of November 11 where the tip of Cape Cod curved like a protective hand around a small bay. As the sailors crawled into the rigging to furl the sails, Master Jones called all the passengers together on the top decks. With him stood Elder Brewster, Master Carver, Master Bradford, and Deacon Fuller—the primary leaders among the Separatists. "These men have something to say," he said.

"Good people," began Elder Brewster. He was bareheaded and his thin, graying hair hung to his shoulders. "There are some among us who think we can afford to go our own ways once we set foot ashore."

Henry and Humility were chasing John Goodman's dogs in and out among the people. "Eliza!" John Tilley ordered under his breath. "Keep thy cousins close to thy apron, dost thou hear?"

Elizabeth grabbed Humility's petticoat and pinched Henry's ear. "Quiet!" she hissed. "I want to hear."

". . . understand thy desire to begin anew,"

Brewster went on, "out from under the burdensome laws of England. But, good people, our survival in this new land depends not on each one going his own way, but on deciding our own future together."

"What art thou saying?" demanded Billington.

William Bradford spoke up. "Among the Brethren, we make our own laws and rules, to which we then willingly submit. We are suggesting this simple democracy to all—both Brethren and Strangers—as a form of civil government for our new colony. All freemen above the age of twenty-one will have a voice in deciding the laws, and a responsibility to abide by those laws once they've been agreed on."

"Hear! Hear!" shouted several voices.

"Let's see a written contract," demanded John Billington. "Then I'll decide if I want to sign it."

The Separatist leaders moved to Master Jones' cabin, where they were provided with parchment and ink. After a time, the men appeared once more, and William Bradford read from the document. " 'In the name of God, Amen. We whose names are underwritten, the loyal subjects of King James . . .' "

Elizabeth strained to hear. She wasn't sure she understood all that the Separatists were saying, but she liked what Master Bradford had said about "all freeman will have a voice." That meant her father and uncle, too, even though they had no land or title.

Bradford's clear voice carried over the whole ship as the people listened. " '. . . do hereby combine ourselves together into a civil body, for our order and preservation; to make just and equal laws, acts, constitutions, and offices, from time to time, for the general good of the colony: unto which we promise all due submission and obedience. . . .' "

When Bradford had finished reading the contract, there was a respectful silence. Then John Carver stepped forward, dipped an ink pen, and signed his name. The other Separatist leaders followed. Captain Myles Standish was the first of the Strangers to sign. Then one by one, all the freemen, both wealthy and poor, both Saints and Strangers, stepped up and signed their names to the document. Even John Billington.

As the freemen were signing, a young voice spoke up. "I'm not a freeman yet." It was John Howland, blushing as usual. "But I would also like to sign my name as my promise to abide by the contract when I have finished my service to Master Carver."

A look of pride and approval glowed in Master Carver's face as his young servant stepped forward and signed his name. Three other servants did the same.

"Good people, thou hast done well," spoke up Elder Brewster. "Having signed the contract, our first order of business is to choose a governor to help us carry out its intent."

"What about Elder Brewster himself?" said William Mullins. Mullins was a shopkeeper, recruited for the colony along with his wife, young son, Joseph, and eighteen-year-old daughter, Priscilla. There were several murmurs of approval.

"Nay, good people," said the older man. "In the absence of our pastor, who remained with the flock in Holland, my responsibilities here are religious, not civil. The man chosen must be a civil servant to all."

Again the people buzzed. Stephen Hopkins was all for nominating a man among the so-called Strangers rather than one of the Separatists. But it was obvious even to Elizabeth that it was the Separatists who had provided leadership in avoiding anarchy and drafting the contract they had just signed.

When all was said and done, Master John Carver was elected as the first governor. This time it was John Howland who beamed with pride and approval.

"Why can't *we* go ashore?" Humility whined.

"Thou hast been ashore," sighed Elizabeth. She and her charges, including two of the Hopkins children, huddled in a corner of the main deck, trying to stay out of the cold wind. Several of the older girls had been sent up to the main deck with a crew of younger children to relieve the congestion below. The Billington boys, Johnnie and Francis, were playing pirates up in the rigging with Henry, Giles Hopkins, and some of the other boys.

"But that was three weeks ago!" Humility pouted. "And all we did was collect wood so Auntie Ann and Auntie Joan and the other women could heat water and wash clothes on the beach."

"And collect mussels," Elizabeth reminded her. The children made sour faces. The shellfish, even when boiled, had made them sick.

"I'm cold," Humility whined. "Can't we go below?"

"Thou knows why." Elizabeth was losing patience. "Mistress White is . . . it's her time." Another baby soon to be born, and still the colonists had no homes.

Winter was nearly upon them, the *Mayflower* was still anchored in Cape Cod Bay, and the passengers were still living on board ship. Captain Standish and sixteen armed men had gone ashore in the longboat a few days after their arrival to do an initial exploration of the Cape. They had wanted to take the shallop, a thirty-three-foot working boat with a small sail, so they could sail along the coastline. But the rough seas had tossed it about during the voyage, so it needed repair before being usable. The explorers had to content themselves with simply going ashore in the longboat and hiking along the narrow cape.

They had returned two days later, having seen no one, but they knew the Indians were about: they had discovered several baskets of corn buried under a small mound, which they had dug up and brought back to the ship. The Separatists praised God for providing food for them in their time of need. But Elizabeth worried, *Wouldn't the Indians be angry that the newcomers had stolen their food?*

Still, the men were in good spirits. Edward Winslow ribbed William Bradford good-naturedly for getting his foot caught in an animal snare set by the Indians. Bradford had stepped right in the noose hidden among the dirt and leaves and—*whoosh!*—he had been pulled upside down by his left foot. The others laughed heartily as they cut him down. Even Dorothy

Bradford allowed a smile when she heard the story.

Now a larger group of men—thirty-four in all, led by Master Jones—had taken the shallop farther along the coast. But the weather was so cold that both shallop and men were soon covered by an icy spray. So most of the men waded ashore. The shallop returned to the mother ship and would pick up the explorers on the fourth day.

But day after day, there was nothing to do but wait and try to keep warm. Almost all the children had a cough or a runny nose—and a good many adults, too.

"Come back here, thou rascals!" Mary Chilton was trying to catch Love and Wrestling Brewster and two of Ellen More's brothers, who were leading her on a merry chase up and down the quarterdeck ladder. Pretty Priscilla Mullins and Desire Minter were telling stories to Ellen More and the Allerton children in another sheltered corner of the deck. "Hey, Freckle Face!" Johnnie Billington teased in Elizabeth's ear as he ran past.

Elizabeth tossed her head and ignored him. Where was Resolved White? she wondered. Probably with Dorothy Bradford. The woman smothered the child, and he wasn't even hers! But now Mistress White would have another baby to occupy her, so maybe it was for the best.

Elizabeth Winslow came up to the main deck. "Mistress White birthed a healthy boy!" she said, smiling at the questioning faces of the four older girls. "She named him Peregrine—'the traveler.'" Mistress Winslow stooped and gathered little Ellen into her arms. "Aye, another wee pilgrim."

Elizabeth woke with a start. She had the feeling that something was wrong. But all seemed quiet in the midnight darkness of the tween deck, except for people coughing in their sleep now and then.

Elizabeth tried to go back to sleep but couldn't. Just that day—December 6—the shallop had set out again with ten colonists and eight crew members on a third exploration, determined not to return until they had settled on a place to set up their colony. But not before Johnny Billington had nearly blown up the ship by shooting off his father's matchlock musket near a barrel of gunpowder that had spilled onto the deck. The fire that had flashed up, causing the children to scream in terror, had been quickly doused by tipping over a precious barrel of beer. The incident had left everyone nervous, but the men prepared to go as planned. They wanted to get beyond the Cape and explore the mainland.

"Please, William, don't go," Elizabeth heard Dorothy Bradford beg her husband. "What if . . . what if Indians attack thee? Let someone else go."

"I must, Dority," Bradford said firmly. "This is why we've come. The sooner we find a place to settle, the sooner I can get thee off this ship and into a proper home. I know it's hard on thee, but God has brought us safely thus far, has He not? We've seen more sign of

*Indians than Indians themselves. They are probably
as frightened of us as we are of them. Now I must go.
Pray that we have good success."*

Dorothy Bradford had watched the shallop a long
time, until it rounded the tip of the small, sheltered
bay where they were anchored and headed across
the larger, open bay to the main shore.

But now Elizabeth lay in the dark, listening to the
soft *slap, slap* of the waves against the ship, and thought
about the Bradfords. Dorothy was still young—maybe
only twenty-one or twenty-two—yet they had a son
who was five. Why, she must have been only fifteen or
sixteen when she got married. Elizabeth snorted. She
couldn't imagine getting married in two more years,
though some girls did. But people got married for a lot
of different reasons, most of them practical. Her sisters, she suspected, got married to get out of the house
when things were bad between her mother and father.
But not her. She wasn't going to marry just any—

There. Another sound, like someone moving
around. Could be just someone getting up to use the
slop pot, but . . . no, it sounded like someone going up
the ladder to the main deck. Elizabeth pulled aside
the curtain of their cabin. In the low glow of the oil
lantern that hung from a beam overhead, she saw a
dark maroon cape disappearing up the ladder.

Mistress Bradford had a cape like that. What was
she doing? Curious, Elizabeth crawled off the sleeping platform and, pulling her blanket around her
shoulders, tiptoed quietly around sleeping bodies

and went up the ladder. At the top of the open hatch, she looked this way and that and finally saw a lonely

figure up on the quarterdeck, a woman, cape pulled around her and dark petticoats blowing in the icy December wind.

Was it Dorothy Bradford? Elizabeth couldn't be sure. She crept along the opposite railing and then around the main mast until she was close enough for a good look. The glow from the lantern below shone through the wooden lattice of the supply hatch at her feet. Yes, it was Mistress Bradford all right. But what was she doing up on the quarterdeck in the middle of the night? Foolish woman. She was going to catch her death of cold up there. And the railing on the quarterdeck wasn't as high and safe as around the main deck.

Elizabeth almost called out and told Mistress Bradford to get in out of the wind. Her mother would! But girls didn't talk to women like that. And Dorothy Bradford didn't look like she wanted anyone to bother her. She was looking out toward the sea. As the ship rocked, she swayed unsteadily and reached out a hand to grasp the rigging. Maybe she was looking for the shallop, hoping her husband would come back soon. But the explorers had just left the day before. It wasn't likely.

Elizabeth shrugged and turned away. If the woman wanted to catch her death of cold up on the deck, then let her. *She* wasn't going to fuss about her. Too many people fussed over Mistress Bradford. Well, other people had problems, too. Weren't they all tired and cold and hungry and lonely? What did she expect out here in the wilderness?

Making her way down the ladder, Elizabeth went back to bed.

Elizabeth usually woke to the psalm singing and prayers of the Separatists up on the main deck, but this morning she heard running feet and a loud commotion. Quickly buttoning her waistcoat, she crawled out of bed. The braziers were cold, and everyone was gathered around the ladder leading up toward the main deck.

"The entire ship has been searched?" Elder Brewster was saying, his kindly face troubled.

"Yes, yes!" cried Mistress Winslow, wringing her hands. "I invited her to sleep with wee Ellen and me since our husbands are away. But when I woke up this morning, she was gone! Dorothy Bradford has . . . simply disappeared!"

Chapter 4

The Secret

A NUMBING DISBELIEF crept through Elizabeth's whole body. Dorothy Bradford was missing? But... that was impossible! She remembered her the night before, up on the quarterdeck, looking sad and alone. Elizabeth had thought she might get ill standing out in the wind, but... missing? Where could she possibly go? The *Mayflower* was anchored in the middle of a cold, lonely bay. Surely she couldn't swim to shore! But if she wasn't on board ship, then where—

"The longboat," someone suggested hopefully.

Elder Brewster shook his

head. "Still tied to the ship. And the exploring party has the shallop. I'm . . . I'm afraid, good people, that we have no choice but to conclude that our dear Mistress Bradford has met with an accident and"—the older man swallowed—"has fallen overboard."

Mistress Winslow looked like she might faint. Several of the women immediately led her to a pile of baggage where she could sit. Sounds of quiet weeping moved through the cluster of passengers gathered around the ladder.

The men, restless, talked among themselves. "Maybe we should search the ship again. Maybe she fell asleep somewhere else and has been overlooked."

"Don't be foolish, man. We searched the ship three times."

"Did anyone see her on deck last night? After she'd gone to sleep in the Winslow cabin, I mean."

"Nay. Master Jones hasn't set a watch at night since we've been anchored in the bay."

Elizabeth, jolted out of her shocked daze, wanted to cry out, "Yes! I saw her! She was walking up on the quarterdeck, looking out at the water. I thought she was very foolish to be out in the bitter wind so late at night." But the words stuck in her throat.

Why? they would ask her. *Why didst thou not tell her to come in from the cold? Why didst thou let her stay out there alone? Why didst thou not wake up someone? Thee knows the quarterdeck rail is lower than the high rail on the main deck. Now see what has happened! Mistress Bradford has fallen overboard—and it's thy fault!*

Stifling the cry of horror that sprang to her lips, Elizabeth staggered back to her family's cabin and crawled into a corner of the short, narrow bed. Curling into a ball, silent sobs shook her whole body.

If she hadn't been so busy criticizing Dorothy Bradford and had been thinking about helping her instead, Mistress Bradford might still be alive.

On the fifth day after Mistress Bradford's disappearance, the exploring party returned. Shouts from the shallop brought everyone running onto the main deck. Elizabeth pulled her wool cape around her shoulders and followed slowly, dreading the awful moment when William Bradford would be told the news about his pretty, young wife.

As the shallop pulled alongside the ice-encrusted *Mayflower*, a rope ladder was thrown down and the exploring party scrambled up, talking excitedly all at once. "We found it!" Edward Winslow grinned, nose and cheeks red from days exposed to cold and wind. "Corn fields already cleared for planting!"

"An abandoned Indian village, I'm sure of it," trumpeted Captain Standish, beaming at his wife, Rose.

"With a freshwater brook that runs right into the sea," said William Bradford. He, too, was smiling through his frost-covered beard and mustache.

"We used Captain John Smith's map," added Governor Carver. "A place he named Plymouth when he explored this area six years ago."

Suddenly, it dawned on the eager explorers that their good news was met with an uneasy silence. "What is it?" asked Edward Winslow, looking from face to face in the silent, shuffling crowd. His eyes alighted on his wife. "Elizabeth?" he demanded.

Elizabeth Winslow put her face in her hands and started to weep.

Governor Carver stepped forward, concern suddenly lining his face. "Pray tell, Brethren," he said, "has something happened?"

Elder Brewster stepped out of the crowd and walked over to William Bradford. He looked tired and older than his fifty-odd years. "William, good man, we have had a great tragedy in thy absence. Thy wife, Dorothy, she . . . she disappeared the night after thee left and is presumed fallen overboard and drowned."

William Bradford blinked as if not understanding what the Separatist leader was saying. The other explorers stood with their mouths open, as if suddenly struck dumb.

Governor Carver was the first to find his voice. "What dost thou mean, 'presumed'? Did no one see her? Is there no trace?"

Elder Brewster shook his head. "We can account for her disappearance no other way. No one saw her, but she must have gotten up in the night for a walk on the upper deck. It was cold and damp that night, and the rigging and outer decks were icy. She must have lost her footing and . . . fallen." The older man laid a hand on Bradford's shoulder. "Her body has not been sighted or found."

William Bradford still had said no word. Looking at his glazed eyes and frozen face, Elizabeth began to tremble. *Thou saw her!* a voice seemed to whisper in her ear. *And still thou hast said nothing!*

Then another voice seemed to drown out the first voice. *Nay!* it scoffed. *Thou didst not see her fall. She was walking in the night when thou saw her. How couldst thou have known she would trip and fall?*

Elizabeth relaxed a little. She should have told Elder Brewster that she saw Mistress Bradford go up on deck that night. Why not? It would only confirm what they already guessed. But she couldn't tell now—not after saying nothing for five days. Still, what did it matter? She didn't see the woman fall overboard. No one really knew what happened. So her death would be a mystery whether she told or not.

Elder Brewster and Governor Carver ushered Bradford, his face still a mask of shock, toward Master Jones' great cabin in the stern of the ship. As everyone watched them go, the first voice again seemed to whisper in Elizabeth's ear:

But thou could have saved her.

The worship on deck that evening, led by Elder Brewster, was more somber than usual, with plaintive hymns about heaven and psalms of comfort. The Tilleys and the other Strangers, unsettled by the untimely death of young Mistress Bradford, joined the cluster on the main deck to pay their respects. William Bradford stood with his hat in his hand as the prayers and hymns were offered, his eyes simply looking out to sea.

"Aye, he's thinking about wee John, back in England, without a mother now," murmured Susanna sadly, clasping little Peregrine to her chest. Resolved clung to her skirts, sucking his thumb unnoticed.

But the next day, attention turned to the report from the eighteen explorers. Many of the men were exhausted and suffering colds and coughs from shivering in the open shallop and camping on the cold, damp ground. The mast of the shallop had broken in three pieces during a sudden squall, nearly swamping the boat; the men thought themselves fortunate to make it to shore using the oars. A few Indians had been seen on shore but had run away when they saw the shallop coming closer. And one morning, as they were reloading the shallop for that day's exploration, strange yells and arrows suddenly began to fly from behind the trees. Several of the Englishmen were able to light their matchlock muskets and fire back at shadowy figures in the trees, but the explorers agreed that both sides probably made more noise than did actual harm. Still, it was their first real contact with Indians, and they named the place First Encounter Beach.

As the explorers rested from their grueling trip, they spread out the crude map charted by Captain John Smith years earlier and tried to point out the place they were suggesting to build their colony. Soon Governor Carver and several other men were deep in discussions about what kind of shelters they should build first, and how many. "Good, good," said Master Jones impatiently. "The sooner thou canst build shelters for thy people, the sooner I and my men can sail for England."

They pulled up anchor on Friday, December 15, and hoisted the sails, leaving the shelter of the small bay at the tip of Cape Cod for the twenty-five-mile trip across the larger open bay. But the winds were against them, and it was Saturday before they once again dropped anchor in a sheltered cove several hundred yards offshore from the small spot on the map marked "Plymouth."

The next day was Sunday, the Sabbath, and even the sailors had resigned themselves to the Separatists' refusal to work on the Lord's Day. Besides, cold and exhaustion were taking their toll on passengers and crew alike, and no one protested the day of rest. Deacon Sam Fuller, a quiet man and the Separatists' Bible teacher, had a small supply of medicinal herbs with him, which he brewed into teas for those suffering coughs and fevers.

Elizabeth brought some tea for her father and uncle, both of whom had gotten chilled on the last exploration and now had hacking coughs. "Thou art kind, daughter," said John Tilley, taking the bowl of tea and swallowing with difficulty. A lump tightened in Elizabeth's throat. If only her father knew how unkind her thoughts had been the night Mistress Bradford—

Elizabeth angrily shook off her thoughts. There wasn't a thing she could do about it now. Dorothy Bradford was dead. She had fallen overboard and drowned. No one knew how; an accident, everyone said. Admitting that she had followed her and seen the young wife and mother standing up on the quarterdeck that night wouldn't change anything. It would have to be her secret.

Chapter 5

The Terrible Sickness

THE *MAYFLOWER* WAS ANCHORED a mile and a half offshore, and the longboat had to ferry the men to the rocky beach each day as the colonists debated exactly where to lay out their town. The plan was for nineteen sturdy, English plank houses to shelter the hundred or so colonists. But first, they would make a common building and a few other buildings so that the *Mayflower* could depart.

On Wednesday, twenty men who were well enough to work went ashore to begin felling trees. Elizabeth glanced anxiously at the gray, threatening skies as she waited for the longboat to come back. A number of women and children were planning to go ashore, to give the children exercise and to collect wood for fuel. Oh! How she longed to stretch her legs and walk about on dry land.

But even before the men had unloaded their tools from the longboat, the surly skies let loose with a driving, cold rain, and they had to turn back.

Swallowing her disappointment, Elizabeth helped her mother get her father out of his wet outergarments and wrapped in a wool blanket. "Oh marry, John! With thy cough, thou never should have gone today," Joan Tilley fussed as she pulled off her husband's wet stockings and rubbed his cold feet. In spite of Elizabeth's disappointment, a tiny smile twitched the corners of her mouth. Her mother's voice was worried, not angry. Coming to the New World was going to be good for the Tilleys. The past was behind them. Now they could build a new life.

"Now, wife, quit thy fussing. I'm all right," said John Tilley. His voice was hoarse, and he winced when he coughed as if his throat hurt. "Eliza, could thou fetch me some of that good tea from Doctor Fuller?"

Doctor Fuller? Amused, Elizabeth craned her neck, searching the tween deck for the gentle deacon. Ever since Samuel Fuller had begun brewing his herb tea for the sick, he had suddenly become "doctor" to the passengers. There . . . she saw him over by the Allerton cabin. Mary Allerton had started labor earlier that morning and was now moaning piteously. Was something wrong? Elizabeth pushed in closer.

"Canst thou not help her, Sam?" Isaac Allerton

was pleading. "I don't want to lose Mary, too."

"I'll do my best, Isaac," said Fuller gently. "But thou must see to the child's burial."

Elizabeth turned away, sudden tears stinging her eyes. Not another death! Not a wee baby, still-born before it ever drew a breath. Suddenly, she felt like someone had pinched out a candle and plunged her spirit into darkness.

The cold rain kept up for four days. Before it was over, Mary Allerton was also buried beside her baby on a little hill beyond the site of the old Indian village the colonists had chosen for their new home. "Marry, what a shame," Joan Tilley said. "Two graves in the ground before even one house on the land."

And one in the sea, whispered the voice in Elizabeth's mind. She shook free of the thought and busied herself mending the toe of her wool stocking.

On board ship almost everyone was sniffling or coughing, and frustration was mounting. Each day brought winter closer with no shelters built yet. Finally on December 24, the rain stopped and the sun broke through. But it was Sunday, and so the colonists remained on board ship for their day of rest and worship—though a number of prayers pleaded with the Almighty to let the weather hold.

Monday, December 25, dawned clear and cold, but not freezing. The Separatists rose at first light, had their prayers on deck, and soon were busily loading axes, saws, shovels, and buckets into the shallop. But a few wives among the Strangers whispered to their husbands and prodded them to speak.

"Uh, Governor Carver," Stephen Hopkins hemmed and hawed, "my wife reminds me that today is Christmas Day."

Christmas! Elizabeth thought. Warm memories flooded through her as she remembered candles flickering at the midnight service welcoming the Christ Child . . . a tasty goose turning over the fire . . . games when she and her sisters were little . . . and on Twelfth Night, the day that celebrated the coming of the Magi, a small gift of lace or ribbon or a few coins.

But Governor Carver continued to pass tools over the side of the ship to those in the shallop below. "That is naught to us, Goodman Hopkins. Christmas is a man-made holiday which we do not celebrate."

Stephen Hopkins cleared his throat. "But we've had a hard journey, Governor. A bit of merrymaking in honor of the Christ Child would do the women and children some good."

"We rested yesterday," Governor Carver said firmly. "Today we must work." A murmur of protest rippled through the Strangers.

Elder Brewster spoke up. "Truly, good people, we honor Christ when He lives in our hearts and we obey His Word day in and day out—not by keeping special days."

"Elder Brewster speaks well," Governor Carver said impatiently. "But our survival is also at stake. No man has the right to make merry out of turn while his fellow man must work. We must all work in the favorable weather. Captain Standish—take several armed men to secure our safety. Bradford— your crew will cut down trees. Winslow . . ."

The work assignments went on. "And, John Alden," the governor added, addressing the young cooper, "enlist as many of the older children and young ladies as can be spared from their normal tasks to dig clay from the banks of the freshwater brook. Not sand or mud; clay."

Elizabeth's disappointment over skipping Christmas vanished. After all, it wasn't as if there was a goose to roast or a place to dance on the crowded deck of the *Mayflower*. But at last! No more just waiting. Now she could actually do something to help build their new homes.

Hunger gnawed at Elizabeth's stomach as she used a flat rock to scrape clay from the banks of the little stream that had been named Town Brook. Her fingers were stiff and cold, her nails broken. Day after day she and the other young people filled buckets with clay and carried them to where the men were framing the twenty-foot-square common house.

In the saw pit, which was about six feet deep, one man stood below a log laid across the opening of the pit, and one stood above. Together they pushed and pulled a long saw, cutting the log into rough planks, which were then fitted into the frame. The clay was

then chinked between the planks to make the house
snug and tight.

Elizabeth struggled to her feet and caught up to Mary Chilton, who was lugging her bucket with slow, dragging steps. "Why do Priscilla Mullins and Desire Minter get to watch the wee ones," Mary complained, "while we dig like pigs in the mud?"

Elizabeth shrugged wearily. "John Alden's probably sweet on Priscilla and doesn't want to ruin her pretty hands." But her heart wasn't in their usual banter. She turned worried eyes to her friend. "How is thy mother, Mary? My father . . . he's truly sick. Couldn't leave the ship this morn. And Mam doesn't look well."

Mary nodded. "Aye. My mother is bad, too. Doctor Fuller says it's probably pneumonia. As soon as the common house is finished, he wants to move the sick there so they can get warm by the fire."

The girls trudged back and forth to the brook two more times before a halt was called for the midday meal. Captain Standish had brought in several wild ducks that morning that had been boiled into a hot soup. Oh! The hot broth felt so good going down Elizabeth's throat. And the roaring bonfire warmed her cold hands and face.

"We should finish chinking the chimney today," Governor Carver said to several of the men. He cast an anxious eye at the sky. "But between the days we lose to bad weather, and those who are too sick to work, the building is going too slow. We must get the passengers off the ship and into shelters."

"We could build temporary huts," William Bradford suggested. "There are a lot of young sap-

61

lings in the woods that could be woven together and then daubed with clay and thatched."

"Mmm, yes. Wattle-and-daub huts," mused the governor. Elizabeth and Mary rolled their eyes at each other. More clay to dig and carry.

That evening, as she climbed into the shallop for the short sail to the *Mayflower*, Elizabeth didn't think she'd ever been so tired. A light, sleeting rain felt like needles against her raw, chapped skin. The other workers hunched like shapeless lumps in their wool capes, watching as the ship slowly grew larger in the blue-gray dusk, wondering how their loved ones on board were faring. Rose Standish was sick; so was Elizabeth Winslow and little Ellen More. William White, the father of Resolved and Peregrine, had been too sick to work today, along with John Tilley and several others.

John Howland and John Goodman went up the rope ladder first, then reached down to help the others up the side of the ship. Elizabeth was too tired to even say thank you. It would just make Howland blush anyway.

In the Tilley cabin, Joan Tilley was trying to spoon some hot broth into her husband's mouth, but he choked when he tried to swallow. And for the first time, Elizabeth saw fear in her mother's eyes. "Take thy wet outergarments off, child," said her mother wearily. "We can't have thee getting sick, too—what? What art thou staring at?"

Elizabeth *was* staring . . . at her mother's mouth. Joan Tilley's gums were swollen and bleeding.

"Doctor Fuller!" Elizabeth cried. "Come quickly!"

Samuel Fuller made his way to the Tilley cabin and gently examined Joan Tilley's bloody mouth. Then he shook his head. "I was afraid this would happen. It often strikes sailors who have been at sea for many months—no one knows why. Though I suspect our poor diet is the cause. Bleeding gums is one of the first signs."

Joan Tilley's mouth trembled. "Signs of what, Doctor?" she whispered.

Again he shook his head sadly. "Scurvy."

The cold, bleak weeks of January and February 1621 were a blur in Elizabeth's mind. One by one, half a dozen wattle-and-daub huts with thatched roofs were built. Slowly, passengers moved off the ship and into the huts. Both the ship and the common house were being used as a hospital for the sick. But there was nothing to do for most of them except hope and pray.

Elizabeth stayed on board ship to tend her sick parents as best she could. But news drifted back from the little village of Plymouth taking shape on the shore. Governor Carver lay sick in the common house. William Bradford took over directing the work crews—but within a few days, he, too, became delirious with fever and could no longer work. So many were sick that Elder Brewster and Captain Standish were helping to cook, bathe, and clean up sickbeds.

Fires burned continuously in the common house fireplace—a crude affair made of wood and clay—to keep the house warm. But twice the thatched roof had caught fire in the middle of the night. Even in their weakened condition, Carver and Bradford had managed to get the others out of the house and saved the barrels of gunpowder. No lives had been lost, but many of the supplies were ruined.

As yet, there had been no encounters with Indians. But the colonists knew they were in the forest, watching. Captain Standish had left tools in the woods while he came back to the clearing for the midday meal. But when he returned, the tools were gone.

When the sickest and weakest ones began to die, the bodies were buried at night on Burial Hill with no stones to mark the site. Pneumonia, tuberculosis, and scurvy—as well as too little food and too much cold and dampness—took their toll. A few small graves were dug for children like little Ellen More and two of her brothers. But most of the graves held hopeful men and brave women who had survived the dangerous ocean voyage, only to die on the shores of the New World: the wife of Captain Standish; Mary Chilton's mother and father; Priscilla Mullins' parents and brother, Joseph; William White, the father of young Resolved and wee Peregrine. Sometimes there were two or three burials in one night.

Everyone knew the reason for the unmarked graves: they didn't dare let the Indians know how weak and few they really were.

And then came the night they wrapped John Tilley's body in a blanket and lowered it into the longboat for the stealthy trip to Burial Hill. A few nights later Elizabeth, numb with grief, watched as her mother's body was gently lowered over the side into the boat. Then she heard the *slap, slap* of the oars as the longboat disappeared into the foggy darkness.

Her eyes stung with hot, unshed tears. *It isn't supposed to be like this!* her heart screamed. *This is supposed to be a new start for all of us—Mam and Father and . . . me.* Elizabeth crumpled into a little heap at the foot of the main mast. She had never felt so alone in her entire life.

How long she lay there, miserable and cold and scared, she didn't know. After a long while, the longboat come back, then someone kneeled beside her. A young woman's voice said gently, "Miss? You can't stay here like this. Mistress Carver says to bring you back to the village with us. You can stay with her until the governor gets well."

Elizabeth raised her head wearily. Desire Minter, the Carvers' maidservant, put an arm around her shoulders. Behind her, John Howland was reaching out a hand. Without a word she let the two servants help her over the side of the ship to the longboat waiting below.

Chapter 6

The Amazing Story

STEPPING OUTSIDE THE CRUDE HUT with a water bucket, Elizabeth was startled to hear the warble of a bird. She stood still and listened. Then she noticed something else: the warm kiss of the sun on her freckles.

Could spring be on its way? It was still early in the year, just a few days into March. The winter had been gray and icy, with sleet instead of snow driving a bone-chilling dampness into everything. But today a warm breeze took the edge off the chilly air, and the blue sky seemed alive with tiny clouds that looked like dandelions gone to seed.

"Good day, Elizabeth," said a pleasant voice. William

Bradford, walking slowly up the slope that led from the beach, paused. "Is Governor Carver within?"

Elizabeth's first instinct was to look away. *If he looks in my eyes, he'll see the secret!* she thought with a flutter of panic. But she forced a polite nod. "The governor's still poorly, but he's up and about. Excuse me, Master Bradford, but Mistress Carver needs some water from the brook."

She scurried across the clearing and down the path to the brook. Now that she was an orphan, Elizabeth thought grumpily, no one called her "Miss Tilley." They called her by her first name, like a servant.

When she returned with the water, Governor Carver and William Bradford were sitting outside the hut, deep in conversation. "The ground didn't freeze deeply," Bradford was saying, "so if this weather holds, we'll be able to start planting in a few days."

Carver nodded thoughtfully. "Good, good. Our people need to put this terrible winter behind them. . . ." His voice trailed off. Then he shook his head sadly. "Half of the colony—wiped out before we begin."

"Yes," Bradford said gravely. "And there are still some, like Ed Winslow's poor wife, who are barely clinging to life."

Elizabeth wanted to stop up her ears. She didn't want to hear about people who had died! Wasn't her own mam, her own father, cold in the ground on Burial Hill? If only she were invisible so she could slip past the Separatist leaders sitting in the doorway.

Bradford sighed. "I don't know, John. Sometimes I think it's just as well that Dorothy—"

"Don't say it, William," Governor Carver said sharply. "It was a tragic accident, and I blame myself that we had no night watch posted."

"Nay, nay, John, don't blame thyself. If anyone's to blame, it is I! I knew she wasn't strong. Perchance I should have left her behind with wee John. But . . ." Bradford sighed again heavily. "At least she didn't suffer this terrible sickness for weeks as many of the women have done. She could not have survived."

Elizabeth's hand clenched the water bucket, and she forced her feet to take her past the two men and through the low doorway into the wattle-and-daub hut. Her heart was pounding. She knew what was happening. They needed someone to blame for Mistress Bradford's death—even if it was themselves. They must *never* know she saw the woman on the deck that night and could have sounded the alarm.

"Thou art dallying, Henry Samson," said Elizabeth crossly. "Just stick the corn kernel in the hole, and let Humility cover it up. Look, Bartholomew and Remember Allerton have almost finished their row."

Henry slumped on the ground, hugging his knees. "I miss Uncle Edward and Auntie Ann," he sobbed.

Elizabeth fiercely poked her sharpened stick in the dirt. "Dost thou not think Bartholomew and Remember miss their mother, too? But we'll *all* die if we don't get this corn planted. Get thyself busy now!" She turned her back and dug another hole, then another. She shouldn't be so hard on her cousins, but she knew if she stopped to comfort them, her own tears would spill over and maybe never stop.

Dig, plant, cover. Dig, plant, cover. It felt good to be outside in the fresh, salty sea air, out of the small, dark huts, digging in the sweet-smelling earth. But for what? she thought. No family, no home—just three orphans in a strange land being cared for by the goodness of strangers. What kind of future was that?

And now Mistress Carver was sick. Elizabeth was glad Desire Minter was there to care for her. She was sick of sickness and felt disgusted by the raspy cough, soiled bedclothes, and dull eyes.

"Eliza," Humility said suddenly, "why are the sailors bringing those big guns from the ship?"

Elizabeth stood up and shaded her eyes from the glare of the sun on the glittering waters of Cape Cod Bay. The *Mayflower* still rode at anchor, waiting for a few more shelters to be built so the last of the sick passengers could come ashore—or die. The shallop was pulled up on the rocky beach, and two heavy cannons—called *minions*—were being unloaded, then rolled on their little wheels up the gentle slope through the single "street" of the crude village.

"They're taking them to the top of Burial Hill, I guess," she said.

"Why?" asked Henry.

"For protection, what else?" Elizabeth said impatiently. From whom or what, she had no idea. She hadn't seen even one Indian yet, and if another ship ever sailed into the bay, it would be a glad sight.

Day after day the planting went on, using the cleared acres from the former Indian village. Beans, peas, wheat—and, of course, the corn seed the explorers had found on Cape Cod. *I'm surprised the Indians haven't attacked us for stealing their corn,* Elizabeth thought uneasily—but she couldn't help but feel glad as first one acre, then two, then three, were planted with the red, yellow, and blue seeds of the "Indian corn." Come next winter, there would be plenty of cornmeal for bread and hasty pudding. If only they had a cow and could have butter and milk with it!

Elizabeth wasn't the only one uneasy about the invisible Indians. Everyone knew the Indians were around; there had been occasional sightings from a distance and signs in the forest. An attack would have been understandable—but why this odd silence?

One day in mid-March, right after the midday meal of cheese, boiled fish, and beans, Governor Carver called a meeting of the twenty men who had survived the sickness to talk about ways to protect the settlement. Elizabeth noticed that even John Howland, the Carvers' indentured servant, joined the men as they gathered in the common house. She shrugged and helped Priscilla Mullins wash up the trenchers—wooden platters for eating—and bank the outdoor cooking fire. Status didn't mean much any more with only ten women—including older girls like herself—still alive. Everyone worked, and worked hard, to keep the struggling colony alive.

The first real house of roughhewn clapboards was going up, and Elizabeth had just organized several of the younger children to gather wood chips for the fire when she saw a strange man come walking through the little village with long-legged strides. Her green eyes widened. His body was long and lean, and his skin glistened golden brown in the sunlight. His black hair hung long and straight down his back but was cut short around his face. The man wore only a leather thong and breechcloth around his waist, and he carried a long bow and a quiver of arrows.

Just then the children saw the strange man, too, and screamed. But he ignored them and strode right up to the door of the common house. Immediately, there was a commotion inside, but Elizabeth heard the man say, clear as a bird call carried on the wind, "Welcome, Englishmen. My name is Samoset."

The arrival of Samoset, walking boldly into their common house and extending his hand in friendship, excited everyone. He was a sagamore, a lesser chief, of an Indian tribe about five days' walk to the north. He had learned to speak some English from ships that had landed along the coast, acting as an interpreter between his people and the white traders and fishermen. But the Englishmen who had landed at Plymouth were building shelters and planting crops; they looked like they were planning to stay, and he had been sent for by the Wampanoag tribe to ask their intentions.

Governor Carver, Bradford, and Brewster were delighted. The Separatists assured the friendly Indian that they wanted to live peaceably with their Indian neighbors. Captain Standish, however, stood to the side and glowered. He didn't trust Indians. He wasn't about to let down his guard just because one heathen spoke a few words of English.

Edward Winslow, however, was eager to learn more about their guest. At the first opportunity, he sat on the ground with the dignified sagamore and tried to learn a few words of his native language.

"Samoset says this clearing used to be a Patuxet Indian village," Winslow reported later to Governor Carver. "But the whole village died of a plague."

"Hmm," said the governor, stroking his chin. "Probably smallpox caught from European sailors."

Elizabeth's neck prickled as she listened from a dim corner of the Carver hut, where she was trying to mend Humility's torn petticoat. Maybe they shouldn't have settled here, clearing or no clearing. Would it always be a place of death?

"He says the sachem or big chief of the Wampanoags is Massasoit, who lives about forty miles southwest of here. He is the one we must convince that we want only peace."

Carver nodded. "Tell Samoset that I would like to meet with the great Chief Massasoit."

Two days later Samoset returned with five Wampanoag men wearing deerskin leggings and moccasins and bringing with them the colonists' tools that had "disappeared" in the forest. Astonished, Captain Standish gave the men a grudging nod of respect. They also brought beaver pelts to trade, but since it was the Sabbath, Governor Carver shook his head. Trading would have to wait for another day.

Two days went by, then Samoset returned. "Chief Massasoit and his people are on their way to Plymouth." The colonists exchanged uneasy glances. Was it a friendly delegation—or an army? They almost didn't notice that Samoset was accompanied by yet another Indian, a tall man with a strong nose and mouth in a craggy face. His head was shaved except for a thick topknot, and he wore a bear claw necklace.

"I am Tisquantum," the man announced in English. "The English call me Squanto. I have been across the sea to thy country of England, and I follow thy religion." An astonished murmur rippled through the little knot of English people. Tisquantum swept a long arm around the clearing. "This land belonged to my people, the Patuxet. When I returned from the long voyage across the sea, all my people had died and the village was no more. The Wampanoag took me in and adopted me as a son. But once more a village is rising on the bones of my people. I have come back to stay." And the man sat down on the ground to show exactly what he meant.

John Billington and Stephen Hopkins exchanged dark looks and hefted their muskets. Captain Standish looked displeased. But William Bradford and Edward Winslow sat down on the ground. "Tell us about thy travels to our country," Bradford said.

In spite of themselves, the colonists, both young and old, crowded closer to their new visitor. Elizabeth gave Henry and Humility a look that said,

"Don't speak out of turn! I want to hear this story."

Calmly, Squanto began his tale. In 1605, an English exploring party had kidnapped Squanto and four other Indians and taken them back to England. As natives of the land English explorers had named "New England," the Indians' information about weather, crops, and inland rivers was invaluable. Squanto had no sooner returned to his own country with Captain John Smith in 1614 when another sea captain, Thomas Hunt, decided that slaves would make a more valuable cargo than fish and fur. Rounding up Squanto and nineteen other Patuxets, he sold them as slaves in Spain. But Squanto fell into the hands of well-meaning Catholic monks, who converted him to Christianity. Making his way to England, he once more set sail for his home in 1619 with yet another sea captain—only to discover that his entire tribe had been wiped out by a plague. Homeless and without a tribe, he had been living with the Wampanoags for the last two years.

"It is good to be home again," said Squanto, looking around the clearing with satisfaction. "But thou will reap only a poor harvest planting in such a way. Squanto can help thee."

"This colony does not *need* the help of a heathen Indian," Captain Standish snapped, grumpier than ever since his wife's death.

"Heathen?" said Bradford amused. "I believe he said he was converted to Christianity."

"Humph," Standish muttered. "This . . . this creature just wants a free meal. Massasoit, now—he's the man we need to be dealing with."

"Perchance thou art right," Bradford said. "But I, for one, am willing to let Squanto dwell with us. This land we stand on was his home, and we need friends."

Elizabeth caught her breath. On the other side of the brook, she saw fifty or sixty Indians come out of the trees and stop. All the men were armed with knives, bows, and arrows.

The colonists had prepared carefully for this important meeting with Chief Massasoit. Soft cushions and even a rug had been laid on the floor of one of the new houses being built. Governor Carver waited out of sight, ready to make a dignified entrance.

Edward Winslow, Captain Standish, and a small militia wearing helmets, armor, and swords splashed across the brook. The other colonists, watching from a distance, could see many gestures back and forth. Finally a tall, muscular Indian in the prime of life, his face painted mulberry red and wearing a deerskin over one shoulder, crossed the brook and strode toward the waiting colonists. He was followed by twenty of his braves, but they had left their weapons behind. All the Indians towered over the squat Captain Standish, who made a show of escorting the chief with his small militia.

"They kept Winslow as a hostage," growled Captain Standish to the waiting colonists.

Within a few minutes, Chief Massasoit and Governor Carver, along with Samoset and Squanto to act as interpreters and as many warriors and English freemen as could squeeze into the unfinished clapboard house, disappeared behind closed doors.

The meeting lasted a long time. When at last the chief and the governor came out, the two men shook hands, and without a word, the Indians waded back across Town Brook and disappeared into the trees. Then Edward Winslow reappeared, unharmed and quite excited about the new words he had learned from Massasoit's men.

"Good people," said Governor Carver as the colonists gathered around him, "today Plymouth Plantation has established a peace treaty with our Indian neighbors. I believe Massasoit desires peace and is a man of his word. We have agreed to do no harm to one another, to come to one another's aid if attacked by enemies, and to punish anyone among us who breaks this treaty. Let us give thanks to God for this important milestone in the brief history of our colony."

The Puritans dropped to their knees, while the other colonists bowed their heads respectfully. But Captain Standish muttered, "Peace treaty? A military alliance is what it is. Massasoit's no fool. He wants an alliance with our guns and cannons to put fear in the heart of his enemies, the Narragansetts. He's using us, just as we're using him."

A few days after the peace treaty with Chief Massasoit on March 22, Governor Carver insisted on holding an election for governor. "Thou elected me governor on board ship," he told the people, "because we needed to organize ourselves before we even set foot on land. But we have now been in our new home four months. By God's grace some of us have survived the winter's terrible sickness. A new year is upon us. It is only right that we have a yearly election from among ourselves as to who should be governor."

Elizabeth knew that the governor was hoping someone else would be elected. She had heard him talking in low tones to his sick wife in the hut after the candles had been blown out at night. He often felt tired, not yet fully recovered from his bout with pneumonia. To no one's surprise, Carver was re-elected governor by unanimous vote.

But that night they buried Mistress Winslow. This time, unafraid of the Indians, the whole colony gathered on Burial Hill while Elder Brewster read a psalm. Elizabeth's throat tightened as dirt was thrown on top of the shroud. Would the dying never end?

Edward Winslow and William Bradford walked down the hill together in front of her. "I'm glad it's over," she heard Winslow say sorrowfully. "I couldn't stand to see my wife suffer anymore. But I regret we never had children. Only our foster child, wee Ellen More, and she's gone, too. I envy you, William. At least thou still has thy son, John."

William Bradford said nothing for a few minutes. Then, "Perchance, Edward. But how do I tell the lad that his mother, whom he waved good-bye to so bravely last summer, is never coming back?"

The last of the *Mayflower* passengers were finally brought ashore. Supplied with some freshly smoked eels and wild duck, Captain Jones pulled up anchor on April 5 and sailed for England.

Elizabeth watched as the square-rigged sails filled with wind. Suddenly, she felt a flutter of panic. The *Mayflower* was leaving. Now they were truly alone!

But she didn't belong here. If Mam and Father were still alive, that would be different. But she was all alone with a group of Puritans she didn't understand, and their only neighbors were nearly naked natives who painted their faces and spoke a strange language.

What if she wanted to go back to England? After all, she had two married sisters. Surely one of them would give her a home. But now it was too late!

The sails on the *Mayflower* grew smaller in the distance. Suddenly, Elizabeth had a great urge to run away. She didn't want to be here at Plymouth! But where would she run? Forests and sky and sea stretched as far as she could see in all directions. She felt as trapped as if she were locked in a small room.

With tears springing to her eyes, Elizabeth started running toward the half-planted fields. She didn't know where she was going, but she had to go somewhere. But as she stumbled half blindly down the path toward Town Brook, Elizabeth thought she heard someone cry out. She halted.

"Help me," gasped a weak voice.

Looking around wildly, Elizabeth saw someone lying crumpled at the edge of the garden only a few yards away. Rubbing the tears out of her eyes, she ran over to the man and knelt down.

"Governor Carver!" she gasped. "What's wrong?"

"Dizzy . . . head hurts . . ." he said weakly. "Get . . . Bradford. Must . . . tell him something."

In an instant, her own troubles forgotten, Elizabeth flew back toward the huts and half-built houses. "Master Bradford!" she screamed. "Come quickly!"

Chapter 7

A Season of Hope

GOVERNOR CARVER AND HIS WIFE were buried within a few days of each other. Probably a stroke, Doctor Fuller had said, and his wife was too ill to survive the shock of it. Elizabeth didn't want to go to the burials. But she was afraid people would think she was being disrespectful since she'd been a member of the Carver household for more than two months. She kept her eyes on the sea as the dirt was shoveled into the graves and tried not to think about the fact that she was once more without "family."

The Separatists did not conduct "funeral services"; in every possible way they tried to distance themselves from the religious pomp and ceremony of the Church of England. At most, Elder Brewster would read a psalm about God knowing our comings and goings. But at Carver's burial, all the men lined up, both Saints and Strangers, and fired a volley of shots in honor of Carver's civil role as Plymouth's first governor.

Squanto and Samoset stood to the side, watching. Seeing the worry in their eyes, William Bradford and Edward Winslow strode over to them. "The treaty Governor Carver made with Chief Massasoit spoke for all of us," Bradford assured them. "We will abide by its terms, even though Governor Carver has been taken from us unexpectedly."

"We meet this very day to elect a new governor," Winslow added.

The meeting in the common house was open to all, though some people had to stand outside the doorway or lean in the windows to hear what was going on. It didn't take long for the colonist freemen to do their business: William Bradford was elected governor, and Isaac Allerton assistant governor.

Standing outside the doorway holding Humility by the hand, Elizabeth saw that Squanto was nodding and grunting his approval. Ever since he had arrived at Plymouth, the craggy-faced Indian had attached himself to Bradford—probably because Bradford had supported his desire to remain with the colonists. Or maybe he sensed in the man what even Elizabeth recognized. Even though William Bradford was twenty years younger than Carver, he had always had an air of quiet authority. She remembered him talking calmly to that annoying Thomas Weston the day the *Mayflower* sailed from England . . . and encouraging each family to exercise their unused muscles after the terrible storms had confined them days on end to their cabins . . . and helping to organize the colonists and do what had to be done to survive the first terrible months in the New World. Yes, Bradford would make a good governor.

Her wandering thoughts were interrupted by Bradford's voice from inside the common house. "I thank thee, fellow pilgrims, for thy confidence," the new governor was saying. "I will serve thee as governor this coming year to the best of the ability God has given me. In spite of our many trials, let us give thanks that our Creator has brought us to this goodly land and given us friends among the native peoples."

A murmur of voices said, "Hear! Hear!" but Bradford continued. "As thy new governor, I have one order of business to conduct immediately—by request of our late governor, Master Carver himself."

Elizabeth's ears pricked up. Carver had sent her running for Bradford, even as he lay dying. What had he wanted to say?

"Before he died, Master Carver told me it was his desire to free his indentured young man, John Howland, from his servitude. And—"

Whatever the new governor intended to say was drowned out in exclamations and congratulations as all eyes turned to the lanky John Howland, whose face flushed red clear to the roots of his hair.

"The governor is not finished!" shouted Isaac

Allerton, flexing his new civil muscles.

When the voices had quieted down, Bradford continued. "As we all know, John and Catherine Carver had no living children. Therefore it was also Governor Carver's wish to leave his estate to this same young man he regarded like a son."

This time astonished murmurs rippled through the assembly. John Billington's face registered total disbelief, mixed with—was it envy? Master John Carver had been a man of "comfortable means" back in England—not that it counted for a great deal here on the other side of the world, where all were working to help one another survive and repay the Merchant Adventurers. Nonetheless, it was highly unusual for a servant to inherit his master's wealth.

"John Howland," Governor Bradford continued, "as governor of Plymouth Plantation and by the authority of King James, I declare thee to be a free man and sole master of John Carver's estate."

A funny feeling prickled all over the back of Elizabeth's neck, where her red curls insisted on escaping from under her coif. Desire Minter, the Carvers' plain-faced maidservant, was beaming at John Howland's good fortune. Beyond Desire, Mary Chilton was trying to ride herd on Isaac Allerton's three motherless children. Elizabeth remembered how often she and Mary had poked fun at John Howland on board the *Mayflower*—they, saucy freemen's daughters, and he an indentured servant who blushed easily. The winter's cold, hunger, and terrible death toll had squelched their silly gossiping. But this . . .

Humility jerked her hand out of Elizabeth's grasp and ran off to play with the other children, leaving Elizabeth with her thoughts a-jumble. So it was *Master* Howland now, heir to the Carver estate. And she, Elizabeth Tilley, was just another orphan in the Carver household. Or was it the Howland household now?

Suddenly, Elizabeth had an urge to laugh hysterically—except she might cry instead. How many more ways could her world flip upside down?

As it turned out, Elizabeth, Humility, and Henry were moved under the protective wings of Elder Brewster and his wife. John Howland might be master of John Carver's estate, but it would have gone against the Puritans' principles to leave a young, unmarried girl in his household. Besides, with the current shortage of housing, it was necessary for Howland to bunk for the time being with the other single men.

Henry was delighted with the change in households. Love and Wrestling Brewster and Richard More—the only one of the More children to survive the sickness—followed him around like younger brothers. "I can't fetch firewood today, Eliza," he told Elizabeth soon after the Brewsters settled in to one of the new clapboard-and-thatch houses. "All the boys have to go to the beach to gather alewives!"

"Alewives! What nonsense is that?" snorted Elizabeth. The tiny, herring-like fish lay dead all over the beach and made it stink.

"Truly, cousin!" protested Henry. "Squanto is teaching us how to get good yield from our corn! He

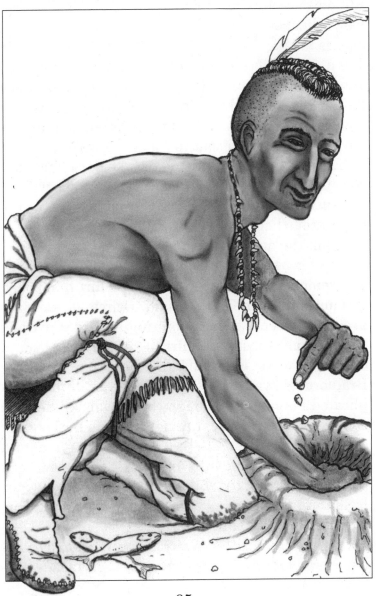

needs all the alewives we can lug to the fields."

This Elizabeth had to see for herself. As the boys ran off to scour the rocky beach for the small, dead fish, Elizabeth picked up the water bucket as an excuse to take the path through the fields that led to Town Brook. "Here comes Freckle Face," teased Johnnie Billington, who was throwing rocks at sea gulls with his brother, Francis. The Billington boys obviously didn't consider themselves among "all the boys" who had been sent to collect alewives.

Elizabeth tossed her head. "Make thyself useful," she shot back. "Get lost in the woods." As she walked on, she looked around guiltily, hoping none of the Separatists had heard her, or she might get a reprimand in the next Sabbath meeting.

Arriving at the corn fields, Elizabeth watched in amazement as Squanto made a little dirt hill, poked in four corn kernels, then laid a circle of alewives around the seeds, heads pointing inward. Covering the fish and seeds with dirt, he swiftly went on to create the next "corn hill." In other rows, Governor Bradford, Edward Winslow, and several others duplicated his method, though the brown-skinned native worked so rapidly that he left them far behind.

"Good day, Elizabeth!" hailed Governor Bradford jovially as he straightened his back. "Thou art just in time with thy bucket. Would thou get us some water from the brook? Trying to keep up with Squanto has whelmed us with thirst!"

The other men laughed good-naturedly and called out, "Aye! Aye!" before returning to their task. Elizabeth flushed at being singled out, but she was glad to have a real reason to head for the brook.

With Squanto's help, the colonists planted twenty acres of corn, beans, peas, and wheat that spring in the fields cleared by the Indian's former tribe. As the weather warmed, building began in earnest on seven sturdy houses, framed in wood and sided with roughhewn clapboard. The steep-pitched roofs were thatched with tightly bound reeds and grasses.

Only three married couples remained of the original eighteen who had boarded the *Mayflower*. In nine families, both spouses died during the sickness; the rest were left widowed. But creating family units in the newly formed society was considered not only desirable, but necessary for its survival. So it was no surprise to anyone when Edward Winslow and Susanna White—who had both been widowed a few months earlier—made known their intention to marry.

"Aye, such a good match," clucked Mistress Brewster approvingly as the Brewster household dressed in freshly washed clothes for the wedding. It was the second week of May, and the simple ceremony would be held in the new common house, which doubled as storage and meeting house. "Little Resolved and wee Peregrine White need a father—and that Edward Winslow is an up-and-coming man."

"But who shall marry them?" asked Elizabeth, giving Humility's long, mousy brown hair a quick brush, then tucking it up under the little girl's coif. "We don't have a clergyman here at Plymouth. Just Elder Brewster." She cast a glance at the balding gentleman who was trying to read a book by the pale light coming through the oiled paper window.

"Aye, my girl," he spoke up, "we pray our good pastor will soon join us from Holland, with others from our congregation. But it matters not as far as the marriage goes. Unlike England, where church and state poke their fingers in each other's business—worse, where one cannot tell the difference between church and state!—here we must keep matters of church and state quite separate. A marriage is a civil contract. The governor will do the marrying. Oh—speaking of Bradford, Mary," he added, speaking to his wife. "I have recommended that he join our household. It is not fitting that our governor bunk with the single men like a common journeyman."

Elizabeth felt the blood drain out of her face. No! She had almost succeeded in burying her secret deep inside, where it did not bother her or whisper accusing thoughts in her ear. But she did not want to live in the same house with the man, to be reminded day after day of that wintry night on the deck of the *Mayflower*. In fact, she did not want to go to the wedding ceremony now. How could Bradford join a man and woman in marriage without reopening the wound of losing his own wife? No, she did not want to see the sadness in his eyes.

Besides taking a wife and becoming instant father to Susanna's little boys, Edward Winslow was also sent several times to visit Chief Massasoit at Sowams with Squanto as guide. Winslow's open, friendly nature made him a natural choice for Plymouth's ambassador.

In return, Chief Massasoit sent one of his own chief warriors, a *pinence* named Hobomok, to live among the colonists. Like Massasoit, Hobomok was a tall, princely man. He brought his wife and children and built a lodge of saplings, bark, and skins a short distance into the woods from Plymouth's stiff line of half-built houses in the open clearing.

"Methinks Squanto is jealous of Hobomok," Elder Brewster said to Bradford as the men and Mistress Brewster sat down for their meal in the "keeping room" of the clapboard house. "His face has looked like a rain cloud ever since this pinence arrived."

Elizabeth set a big pot of bean porridge in the middle of the table along with small baked loaves of "one-third" bread made from coarsely ground wheat, rye, and corn flours. Then she poured mugs of weak beer for everyone. The five younger children stood around the table, dipping their bread into the pot of beans, listening with big eyes. The Indians were endlessly fascinating, especially to the boys. But Elizabeth tried to be as inconspicuous as possible whenever Governor Bradford was around.

"Thou noticed?" Bradford said with an amused smile. "No doubt he thought he spoke for Massasoit until Hobomok arrived. As for myself, I am glad for both their presence. We need all the friends we can get among the native peoples here. Squanto already has proved to be a valuable friend. I think he trusts me, as I do him. But Captain Standish seems more trustful of this Hobomok; they think alike. They are a good match."

Suddenly, Elizabeth was aware of a commotion outside. "Governor! Governor Bradford!" cried a woman's voice, high-pitched and shrill. Billington's wife burst through the doorway, which was open to the late June sunshine. "Many pardons, Mistress Brewster . . . Elder Brewster," she gasped. "But it's my Johnnie. He went out into the woods hunting for squirrels betimes this morn but hasn't returned. Oh marry! What if those heathens—"

"Calm thyself, good woman," said Governor Bradford. "Surely it is not time for concern. It is only midday."

Chapter 8

Medicine Girl

BY NIGHTFALL, JOHNNIE BILLINGTON had not returned, and a search party had found no trace of the boy. "Governor," said Captain Standish, reporting to the Brewster house, "I suggest sending Hobomok to Chief Massasoit, asking for his help. The chief knows all the tribes in this area. His scouts will soon learn if any of the Indians have taken the boy."

Curled up in the trundle bed with Humility that night, Elizabeth tried to silence the voice that whispered in her mind. *Thou told Johnnie Billington to get lost in the woods,* the voice whispered. *I didn't mean it,* she argued with herself. *But he's such a horrid tease about my freckles.* It was a long time before she fell asleep.

The next day another search party went out. Restless, Elizabeth finished her chores quickly and slipped away by herself. The Brewsters were good to her, but she couldn't help feeling like a stranger or just one of the servants. She didn't really *belong* in the family. In fact, she didn't really *belong* at Plymouth Plantation. Here she was, fourteen years old now and almost an upgrown woman. But she was nobody. She didn't really matter to anyone anymore. Maybe . . . maybe this was her punishment for thinking unfriendly thoughts about Mistress Bradford— and now Johnnie Billington. She tried to tell herself it wasn't her fault the boy got lost in the woods, but she still felt guilty for *wishing* he would.

"Oh!" she said, startled. Without realizing where she was going, she had walked right into Hobomok's family camp. Hobomok's wife was sitting under a sun shelter—a woven mat stretched between four poles—weaving a tight, neat basket with twisted river reeds.

The woman was wearing a deerskin wrapper tied around her waist and a seashell necklace. Her black hair was cut short in front but hung long down her back. She looked up at Elizabeth and smiled, showing her stained teeth. With a nod of her head, she invited Elizabeth to sit down. Several children, naked except for waistcloths, stood nearby, staring at her freckles and the wisps of red hair that escaped from under her coif.

Elizabeth watched intently as the Indian woman finished the basket. How light and useful that basket must be! Unlike the heavy wooden or metal bowls and buckets the colonists used. Could she learn how to make a basket like that?

When the woman was finished, she got to her feet and with a smile beckoned Elizabeth to come with her. The children skipped around them as they walked into the woods. Stepping carefully among the tangle of vines, wild flowers, and bushy plants that covered the forest floor, Hobomok's wife cut bunches of a fernlike leaf with her knife and put them in her basket. Elizabeth noticed that the plant had a lacy, lavender-colored flower that looked similar to Queen Anne's lace. Seeing Elizabeth's curious face, Hobomok's wife sliced the air with her knife, as if cutting her forearm. Then she winced as if in pain, pointed to the fernlike leaves in her basket, and made a gentle rubbing motion on her forearm.

"Oh!" laughed Elizabeth, understanding. "Thou makes a salve from the leaves of that plant for cuts and wounds." Elizabeth made the same gentle rubbing motion.

Hobomok's wife smiled broadly and nodded. Next, she plucked the leaves of a plant that looked similar to dandelion leaves and faked a gagging cough. The children giggled at their mother's playacting.

With delight, Elizabeth recognized the next plant: chamomile, its delicate leaves spreading low and wide, almost like a ground cover. She held her own

tummy and groaned, then pointed to the chamomile,
pretended to drink it as a tea, and sighed happily,

sending the Indian children into even greater fits of laughter.

But she didn't recognize the next plant, which had medium-long leaves branching out from stalks that bent over gracefully. Hobomok's wife laid her head to the side on her flattened hands and closed her eyes, as if falling asleep. Elizabeth grinned. A sleeping herb.

Back at their campsite, Hobomok's wife tied the herbs in small bunches and hung them from a leather thong to dry—but not before giving Elizabeth several bunches of each one to take home with her. Then she pointed to herself. "Nooma," she said.

Excited, Elizabeth ran all the way back to the Brewster house with her treasure. Mistress Brewster and Deacon Fuller were seated at the table in serious conversation when Elizabeth ran inside.

"See what I—" she started to say excitedly, but Mistress Brewster jumped up.

"Where hast thou been, Elizabeth Tilley!" she cried. Her voice sounded half cross, half relieved. "The afternoon is gone, and I was just about to send out a search party for *thee!*"

Elizabeth's mouth dropped open. Had she been gone so long? "I . . . I only meant to go for a short walk, but Hobomok's wife, Nooma, why, she showed me how to find herbs in the woods for cuts and coughs and tummy aches!" She held out the bunches of herbs.

But Mistress Brewster scarcely noticed. "Shame on thee, girl, talking folly with heathens instead of tending to thy duties. Why, no sign of poor, lost Johnnie Billington yet, the men all out searching, the lad's mother nigh to fainting with worry, and thou art playing in the woods! Hurry now, wash thy hands and start laying out the supper."

Her face burning, Elizabeth turned to the water bucket sitting on a bench and dipped water into a basin. Behind her she heard Deacon Fuller clear his throat and say, "Forgive me, Mistress Brewster, might I have a word?" Stools scraped and their footsteps carried them outside.

Tiptoeing to the door, Elizabeth saw that Fuller and Mistress Brewster had stepped to the corner of the house. By straining, she could just barely hear what Deacon Fuller was saying.

"I recognize some of the herbs the girl had— yarrow, sweet rocket, and valerian. These would be very useful to add to the small store of herbs and medicines I have. But surely thou can see that it would be awkward for me to spend time with Hobomok's wife, learning her plant wisdom. But if the girl has taken an interest in herbs—"

"Oh marry, Deacon Fuller, dost thou really think it's a good idea?" protested Mistress Brewster. "We don't want to turn the girl into an Indian 'medicine girl' herself. And what about her other tasks?"

Deacon Fuller was persistent. "I pray thee, think on it, mistress. We must learn from our Indian friends if we hope to survive in the New World. Elizabeth's knowledge of their healing herbs could be useful to us all."

◈ ◈ ◈ ◈

The colony had almost given up hope when Massasoit finally sent word that his scouts had located the Billington boy—alive. After wandering in the woods for several days with only berries to eat, the boy had stumbled into an Indian village at the base of Cape Cod, and from there had been sent to a tribe of Nauset Indians farther up the Cape nearly to the place where the *Mayflower* had first anchored.

"That's the area where we found the buried Indian corn," Elder Brewster mused. "Dost thou think they are holding the boy for revenge?"

"I know not," Bradford said grimly, putting food in a pack for the journey. "But we promised ourselves before God we would repay what we took to save us from starving. Though we can ill afford it until we harvest the crops, we must try to make our peace." They loaded the shallop with baskets of corn the colony had gotten in trade from the Wampanoags, plus gifts of cloth, knives, and beads. Then the governor set sail across the bay with Captain Standish, Hobomok, Squanto, and a small crew.

Elizabeth was glad to hear that Johnnie Billington had not died in the woods. But she was gladder still that Mistress Brewster relented and allowed her to visit Hobomok's wife to learn about local herbs and their uses. Herb lore was like a puzzle: learning how to spot the various plants from among the wild tangle in the forest, figuring out from Nooma's sign language how they were used, then showing the herbs to Deacon Fuller for him to look up their English names in his herb book. Each day there was something new to learn: drying the herbs, making some into salves, others into teas or syrups, using still others to flavor stews and vegetables.

Johnnie Billington had been gone several weeks when the shallop finally returned, the rescue mission successful. Henry and the other boys stood open-mouthed as Johnnie climbed out of the shallop, decked out from head to toe with Indian *wampum*— necklaces, bracelets, and anklets made from fine white shells. He fought off his mother, who tried to smother him in hugs, and swaggered up the hill followed by a crowd of young admirers peppering him with questions.

Elizabeth rolled her eyes at Mary Chilton: If Johnnie Billington was a pain before, now he would be unbearable!

But learning about herbs from Hobomok's wife brought Elizabeth a measure of happiness that summer of 1621. She had somewhere else to go when living in close quarters with William Bradford in the Brewster household threatened to awaken her sleeping secret, and it gave her something new to fill her restless mind. And "Doctor" Fuller's enthusiasm for her new skill made her feel like something more than a kitchen maid and nanny. "This plant belongs to the lavender family," he'd muse. "Thou says Nooma brews the leaves for snakebites?" Or he'd ask incredulously, "Thou saw Nooma mix a poultice of wild carrot tops with honey, and it stopped the running sore on her little boy's leg?"

In late summer, the colonists brought out their sickles and began harvesting the fields they'd planted. Ears of corn from the fields Squanto had helped them plant soon filled all the baskets and sacks they could gather, and John Alden was kept busy making new barrels. The wheat and pea crops were disappointing, but the bean harvest looked promising, and a fair number of pumpkins, squash, carrots, onions, cabbages, and potatoes helped fill the storehouses. The shadow of starvation that had hung over the colony during the miserable winter disappeared in the sunshine of Plymouth's first successful harvest.

By the time the tree leaves began turning gold and red, seven sturdy clapboard houses with thatched roofs—each with one all-purpose room and a loft—had been completed along the "main street" of Plymouth Plantation, as well as the common house and three storage sheds. By order of the governor, heads of household were assigned: Elder Brewster; John Billington; Isaac Allerton; Edward Winslow; Francis Cook; Peter Browne; and John Goodman. The rest of the families, single men and women, orphans, and servants were divided up among the seven households without regard for who were Separatists and who were not.

"Goodwife Hopkins is upset because her husband was not assigned head of household," Mistress Brewster clucked as the Brewster household dipped into a savory pot of stew flavored with marjoram, basil, sorrel, and parsley that Elizabeth had picked in the woods.

"Then let her take comfort that our own governor"—Elder Brewster looked meaningfully at William Bradford—"assigned himself nary a house, as well." It offended the older man's sense of decency that their elected governor was still sleeping in his loft with the little boys.

Bradford smiled. "More houses will be built in time. But, dear friends, think! Less than a year ago we set foot in this wilderness. Yet today our storehouses are full, we have peace with our Indian neighbors, our new homes have sturdy roofs and warm fireplaces against the coming winter. It would not be unseemly to set aside a day just to give thanks—"

"A party!" squealed Humility—then clapped her hand over her mouth as all eyes turned to her. Children were supposed to be seen and not heard at the supper table while the grown-ups talked.

But a party it turned out to be. All the colonists cheered the idea of a day of thanksgiving and decided to invite their Indian friends to a great feast. On the appointed day in mid-October, Chief Massasoit showed up with ninety of his braves plus women and children, and five deer to roast over the open fires.

The celebration lasted three days. Venison, fish, rabbit, and wild fowl were roasted and eaten with great relish, along with corn bread, puddings, stews, and what little butter and cheese the colonists had left from their ship's stores. The Indian women looked on with interest as the Englishwomen laid out the food they'd prepared, and both white and brown children dodged in and out of their elders playing chase and tag.

On the second day, Elizabeth and Mary Chilton took advantage of the holiday from normal chores to walk arm in arm behind the row of houses to where the men were showing off their skills shooting targets. The colonists fired their matchlock muskets, which were slow and clumsy but made an impressive noise and shot a great distance. The Indian warriors in turn pulled back their taut bows and sent arrow after arrow thudding into the mark.

"Oh marry," groaned Mary. "Captain Shrimp is going to parade the militia up and down the street again."

"He's making sure the Indians are impressed," said Elizabeth dryly.

"I doubt it's the Indians he's trying to impress," Mary giggled. "Did thou not see him making eyes at Priscilla Mullins at the feast yesterday?"

Elizabeth's eyes widened. Nineteen-year-old Priscilla caught the eye of all the young single men, and it was only a matter of time until someone spoke for her hand in marriage. But surely not Captain Standish! True, he was a widower now and needed a wife as much as any man, but—

"Mistress Brewster wants thee, Elizabeth!" Henry shouted, galloping past with a pack of boys as happy and carefree as puppies. The girls sighed and hurried back to help set out food for the day's feast.

When all was ready, Elder Brewster and Deacon Fuller led the colonists and their guests in prayers of thanksgiving. Elizabeth listened intently. She still wasn't used to hearing prayers outside of the formal ritual of the Church of England. But the Puritans prayed with arms upraised or down on their knees as if they were really talking to God. Even Governor Bradford prayed, removing his hat and lifting his face heavenward, thanking God fervently for His many mercies in saving their lives and giving them shelter and food to eat.

As she listened, Elizabeth felt confused. She wished someone would explain more about God and what the Separatists believed about Him. She *wanted* to be thankful, but wasn't it selfish to be grateful for God's mercies for yourself when not all the *Mayflower* passengers had lived long enough to receive those mercies, too?

Chapter 9

Fortune and Misfortune

THE LEAVES HAD FALLEN from the trees, and November rains had soaked the harvested fields when the colonists sighted a sail on the horizon. No ship had sailed into the bay since the *Mayflower* set sail in April, and it brought all the colonists out of their houses and away from their tasks to look and wonder.

"English or Spanish?" growled Captain Standish. "Or maybe French. Humph. Just like the French to let us hack out a plantation here in the wilderness, and then try to take it over." Not wanting to take any chances, the captain ordered all the men to load their muskets and posted several men on the hill with the loaded cannons.

But finally one of the sharp-eyed boys

yelled out, "I see the Union Jack!" Excitement rippled through the colony. "Praise God! An English ship," some cried. "The Merchant Adventurers have finally sent us supplies!" Others breathed a prayer of hope that some of the loved ones they'd left behind would be on the ship.

The ship was named the *Fortune*, and the colonists sent out their shallop to meet it. When the shallop returned, the Brewsters nearly wept with joy to see their oldest son, Jonathan, a young man of twenty-eight. "And thy sisters?" cried Mistress Brewster. "Are they—"

"They are well, Mother," said Jonathan. "And they hope to join you when Fear finishes her education."

All day long, the shallop ferried passengers ashore. Thirty-five men, women, and children had come to join the colonists, including some of the Separatists who'd been left behind when the *Speedwell* began leaking, and the wives of two of the men who had come on the *Mayflower* alone.

Elizabeth saw no one she knew. Her heart sank. Thirty-five more strangers to squeeze into the seven clapboard houses. Around her, the colonists tried to be welcoming, but Elizabeth could see in their faces that many had the same thought.

"Well, well, are all ashore?" boomed William Bradford heartily. "If so, let us send back the shallop to start unloading the supplies thee has brought."

The faces of the newcomers were blank. Jonathan Brewster cleared his throat awkwardly. "The ship has naught in the way of supplies, Governor."

There was a stunned silence on the beach, with only the waves chattering on the shore. Finally Governor Bradford found his voice. "The Merchant Adventurers were supposed to restock our supplies with the next ship from England! We need farm tools and more gunpowder, knives, pots, and beads to trade with the Indians, as well as flour, butter, cheese, candles—"

"And cloth." Susanna Winslow's voice was a desperate plea. "The children's clothes are mere rags!"

Bradford's jaw clenched. "At least . . . surely thou has brought food enough for this company to feed thee through the winter."

Jonathan shook his head miserably. "The ship has been four months at sea. We were much relieved to finally see land, for our food supplies were all but gone."

The colonists looked at one another in dismay. Thirty-five more mouths to feed, but no additional food? Suddenly, the stored crops the colony had hoped would feed them until next year's harvest seemed to shrink.

"But I do have several letters addressed to thee, Governor—one from Thomas Weston," Jonathan Brewster said hopefully. "Maybe it will explain." He withdrew two sealed packets from his waistcoat.

Bradford curtly nodded his thanks. "First things first," he said. "We must get these good people assigned to houses so they might have shelter from this cold wind."

It took the rest of the day to sort the new people and their simple belongings into the seven houses. "We may need to move some of the unmarried men into the storehouses," Bradford mused to Elder Brewster that night as a light drizzle and cold wind whined outside the snug house.

Elizabeth pretended to be asleep in the trundle bed, but it was impossible not to eavesdrop in the crowded house. She heard Bradford break the seal on the letters brought by the *Fortune*.

"This is good news," he said. "The Council on New England has accepted the Mayflower Compact that we all signed in good faith and has issued a new patent making Plymouth Plantation a legal colony."

"Praise be to God!" exclaimed Elder Brewster. "Now—what does that rascal Thomas Weston have to say?"

There was silence in the flickering candlelight. Then Bradford sucked in his breath angrily. "He says they sent no supplies because we sent the *Mayflower* back with her cargo holds empty—and he accuses us of being lazy and poor managers."

Elizabeth couldn't believe her ears. She wanted to scream, "Doesn't he know how many people *died*?" But she didn't have to because Elder Brewster exploded.

"Lazy? Poor managers? Doesn't that ridiculous man know that it took every ounce of strength and the grace of God just to stay alive from day to day last winter? That it took months to even meet the Indians, much less establish a peace treaty and begin trading? Why, that ignorant, pompous—"

"Hush, husband," shushed Mistress Brewster. "Thou wilt wake the children."

The voices around the flickering candle lowered. But as Elizabeth drifted into a fitful sleep, she heard William Bradford sigh heavily. "We have no choice. We must fill the holds of the *Fortune* as best we can to fulfill our contract with the Merchant Adventurers. At least we have one resource in plenty which England lacks—wood!"

When the *Fortune* sailed in mid-December, its cargo holds were full of split cedar clapboards— "Wood we should be using to build more houses," Stephen Hopkins and several others complained—as well as dried fish and two barrels full of beaver pelts worth five hundred pounds English money. The colonists had traded whatever personal and household things they could do without to get the furs.

Several times, seeing the *Fortune* anchored in the bay, Elizabeth had thought about asking someone to write a letter to her sisters back in Bedfordshire. But she felt tongue-tied about asking Governor Bradford for permission to return to England. She avoided him as much as was possible living in the same house, keeping the younger children out from under foot and serving food at mealtimes without speaking. And Deacon Fuller had been keeping her busy making salves and stomach teas and cough syrups from Nooma's herbs for the thirty-five newcomers who were sickly, weak, and underfed from four months at sea.

Then one day, the *Fortune* was gone.

Sitting in the crowded common house a few days later for Sabbath meeting, the feeling of being "trapped" again in the middle of this great wilderness threatened to overwhelm her. But, Elizabeth tried to reason with herself, more people were coming to help settle the new colony. There were unmarried young men among the passengers from the *Fortune*, and she was getting older. Maybe someday someone like John Howland would need a wife and—

Elizabeth felt her face go red. *Why* in the world was she thinking "someone like John Howland"? Embarrassed, she had to admit to herself she often watched him in Sabbath meetings or took notice when he walked past the Brewster house on the way to the fields or down to the shore. He seemed more rugged and confident since he had become his own master. He was good-looking in a sturdy way, but he never seemed to notice her.

The afternoon sermon was drawing to a close when Hobomok appeared in the doorway of the common house and signaled urgently for Governor Bradford to come outside. As the rest of the worshipers filed out into the damp December chill, Elizabeth saw a delegation of unfamiliar Indians standing cold and unsmiling in front of William Bradford. They handed the governor a bundle of arrows wrapped in snakeskin.

Bradford turned to Hobomok. "Can thou tell me

the meaning of this?"

"Narragansett warriors," Squanto butted in. "They bring snakeskin challenge from their sachem, Canonicus. It means fight."

Captain Standish and a few of the other colonists tightened their grip on their muskets as Bradford looked thoughtfully at the snakeskin. Then the governor unwrapped the arrows, laid the snakeskin on the ground, and called for some gunpowder and buckshot. Wrapping the powder and shot in the skin, he stood up and handed it back to the Narragansett warriors. "Tell thy sachem we desire peace. But if he attacks us first, we will fight."

When Edward Winslow translated the governor's meaning, the warriors turned on their heels and disappeared into the forest.

The colonists buzzed among themselves. What did this mean? Would there be war? Even adding the newcomers, there were still fewer than fifty men at Plymouth.

"Send for Chief Massasoit," John Billington demanded. "Our treaty says he must come to our aid if we are attacked."

"Calm thyselves," said Governor Bradford, raising his voice. "We do not want to give Canonicus reason to believe we are preparing for war. If a fight looks unavoidable, then we will send for Massasoit."

"But this challenge proves we must take more steps to defend ourselves," Captain Standish said hotly. "I say we build a stockade fence around our village and post a watch at night so that we are not taken by surprise."

"Hear! Hear!" agreed several voices.

"Build a stockade?" Stephen Hopkins protested. "But that could take months! What about the new houses? We are crammed so tightly in these wooden cages, we can scarce breathe!" But Hopkins was quickly overruled, and work began on the stockade the very next day.

As winter settled in along Cape Cod Bay, all the men who could be spared from hunting, fishing, and chopping firewood went into the woods to cut sturdy poles for the fence. Elizabeth noticed that Governor Bradford worked alongside all the other men, chopping, stripping bark, tying together the eleven-foot-high stakes. Every day except the Sabbath, work continued on the stockade, and it slowly grew in a large oblong from the top of Burial Hill, down toward the beach, then back again, leaving room for many more houses to be built. Christmas Day, 1621, was like any other work day, with the usual amount of grumbling among the Strangers.

But no one saw any sign of the Narragansetts. Bradford's reply to the snakeskin challenge had been heard—and understood. It was a good thing, because the colonists had enough troubles to deal with. Food was running low, and the governor had to cut everyone down to half rations. At the earliest sign of spring, the women and older children went into the fields to begin planting.

One day as the stockade neared completion, Henry came running from the woods. "Where's Deacon Fuller?" the boy yelled at Elizabeth. She and Priscilla Mullins were seasoning a large pot of beans over an open fire for the workers' midday meal. "Accident! John's bleeding bad!"

Priscilla's face paled. "Not . . . John Alden."

"Nay, John Howland! Near cut off his leg with an axe!"

Without a word, Elizabeth went running to find Deacon Fuller, and by the time she found him, John Howland had been carried in from the woods to the common house, his breeches and wool stockings soaked bright red with blood. Quickly Deacon Fuller peeled off the young man's clothing and saw gratefully that the leg was still firmly attached. But the axe had bounced off an icy tree and cut a deep gash in Howland's calf.

Deacon Fuller was now used to having Elizabeth as an assistant when he tended the sick. He automatically asked her to fetch clean rags, wash the wound, and bring him a needle and waxed thread to stitch up the gash—even though she tried several times to slip away. She couldn't bear to look at John Howland's white face, twisted with pain, as the colony's "doctor" stuck a sewing needle into the quivering flesh.

When the bleeding had been stopped, Deacon Fuller said crisply, "Elizabeth, how much yarrow salve do we have to put on the wound?"

"It . . . it's almost gone," she stammered. "B-but— Nooma has a big supply of wild d-daisy, which the Indians use to stop infection."

"Good. I want you to come here twice a day and change this dressing, putting some fresh salve on the

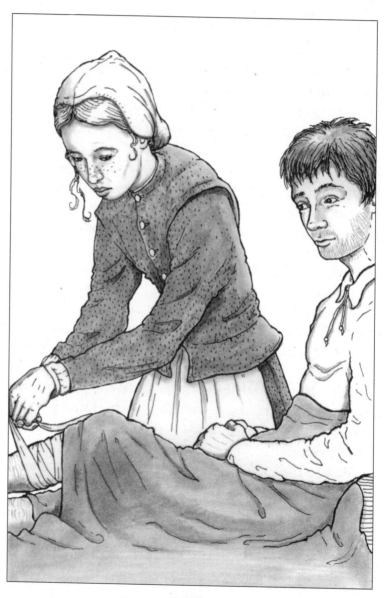

wound. Do you understand?"

The girl nodded mutely, but she wanted the earth to open up and swallow her.

Elizabeth dreaded the twice-a-day visits to the common house. She was sure John Howland could see her heart beating rapidly under her waistcoat as she unwound the old bandage, rubbed on the salve, and wrapped the leg again. But she needn't have worried. He rarely looked at her, and though he was polite, he said little.

One day as she was rewrapping the wound, she heard Nooma's oldest boy calling to her outside the common house. " 'Liza-bet, come! More daisy. Mama give."

"Come on in, Meeka,"

"No, no! No want bad sickness in box under ground. You come get."

Puzzled, Elizabeth went to the door. The boy looked frightened. She tried to ask what he was talking about, but he thrust the herbs into her hand and ran off.

John Howland was struggling to his feet when she came back. "Help me outside, please, Miss Tilley," he said. "Methinks I'll go crazy cooped up in here like a sack of flour."

Startled, Elizabeth forgot about Meeka and his strange talk about "sickness in a box." John Howland just called her *Miss Tilley*! But when her patient sank gratefully to a stool outside the door and said nothing more, she scolded herself. He meant nothing by it; just old habit.

❖ ❖ ❖ ❖

The stockade with its four gates—top of the hill, facing the sea, and one on each side—was completed in early spring. All the men were divided into squads and a general watch was posted day and night. Some of the men thought it was a waste of time—until the day a young, unarmed warrior came running through the north gate, his face bloody and pointing wildly behind him.

"What is he saying?" Captain Standish demanded, turning to Edward Winslow.

"Says he's Wampanoag," Winslow said, frowning. "He ran into Massachusetts warriors, says they're marching this way to attack, came to warn us. But . . . strange. I've never seen this man before."

Squanto and Governor Bradford were quickly summoned. "I was afraid this happen," Squanto said gravely. "Chief Massasoit pretending to be thy friend, while secretly telling Massachusetts to attack. Squanto will stop them. Must go now." With that, the tall, lean Indian strode out the gate, taking the stranger with him to show him the way.

Governor Bradford looked dumbfounded. "But I trusted Massasoit! Where's Hobomok? I must talk to him immediately."

Captain Standish frowned suspiciously as Squanto disappeared into the woods. "Hobomok went to see Chief Massasoit. He told me privately he has heard rumors that we are hiding a horrible plague in a box and plan to let it loose among the Indian tribes.

He suspects Squanto—"

"Marry!" Bradford steamed. "Well, until we sort this out, we cannot take chances. Bring everyone inside the stockade, close the gates, arm all the men, and post them around the stockade."

The day passed uneasily, and a watch was posted all night. But the next morning a lookout called out, "Squanto coming—alone!"

The north gate was opened, and Squanto greeted Governor Bradford and the other leading men triumphantly. "All is well!" he said. "Squanto convince Massachusetts to lay down weapons and come in peace, talk trade instead."

"Well done, Squanto!" Bradford said, relief easing the worry lines in his forehead.

While Squanto told his story, another lookout yelled, "Hobomok comes—with eight, maybe ten of Massasoit's men!"

When Hobomok saw Squanto, anger flashed from his dark eyes. "Squanto traitor to peace treaty!" he said. "Trying to make himself big in English eyes. Massachusetts no plan attack; they come to trade. Squanto also try to make Indians afraid. Tell my son, tell others that English have bad sickness hidden in box in common house. Chief Massasoit say traitor must die!"

The colonists looked stunned. What was going on here? Squanto's face hardened, and he stepped back until Governor Bradford and the others were between him and Hobomok's men.

Another Wampanoag warrior stepped forward.

"Massasoit demand Squanto's head and hands as proof that traitor is killed as agreed."

Governor Bradford didn't move. He seemed caught in a trap. Everyone knew he had befriended Squanto, even when others didn't want to. Would he have to choose between loyalty to his friend and honoring Massasoit's demands?

Just then one of the lookouts yelled, "A sail! A sail in the harbor!"

All eyes turned to the sea. Bradford reacted quickly. "I will deal with Squanto later," he told Hobomok and the other warriors. "But now we must determine whether this ship is friend or foe and prepare to meet them." With that he turned on his heel and strode down the main street of Plymouth toward the east gate. Squanto, Captain Standish, and the other colonists were close behind, leaving Massasoit's warriors standing with their mouths open.

Chapter 10

News From England

THE SAIL IN THE HARBOR turned out to be a shallop from an English ship fishing down the coast. Seven of Thomas Weston's men waded ashore and informed Governor Bradford that they intended to start a new colony farther north. They presented a letter from Weston asking Governor Bradford to "feed and house" them until they could get settled.

"The nerve of that man!" Mistress Brewster fumed, scrubbing the ears of Love and Wrestling that night before sending them to bed in the loft. Elizabeth performed a similar chore on Richard More and Henry. "He sends more mouths to feed and nothing to feed them with."

Elder Brewster watched Bradford, who was pacing back and forth on the packed dirt floor of the clapboard house. Finally he asked, "Whatever happened to Massasoit's messengers?"

William Bradford halted. "By God's mercy," he gasped. "I forgot all about them." He would have rushed out the door, but Henry pulled his head away from Elizabeth's firm grasp and piped up, "Begging thy pardon, Governor. But the warriors left hours ago. They looked very angry."

Bradford sank onto a stool with a short, painful laugh. "I never thought we'd be trying to keep peace *between* the Indians. But I'm not willing to kill Squanto. Despite his foolish treachery, he has been our friend. I must find another way to smooth Massasoit's ruffled feathers, for we cannot lose his friendship, either."

The governor put his head in his hands as Mistress Brewster and Elizabeth hustled the younger children to bed. Weston's letter lay on the table before him. Finally he looked up at Elder Brewster. "Weston says the *Fortune* was attacked by French pirates and stripped of all her cargo before reaching England. It means starting all over again repaying our debt to the Merchant Adventurers." He sighed heavily. "I am calling a meeting of all the Brethren and Strangers tomorrow. We must all work harder if we hope to make it through the next year."

✧ ✧ ✧ ✧

John Howland's leg healed well, though Elizabeth noticed he limped a bit at the end of a day's work. But she had little time to think about Howland's troubles, much less her own. Plymouth was in crisis. By June, the colony's supply of corn was gone and the new crop was not yet ready to harvest. Then a fishing vessel brought news that Indians had massacred many whites in Virginia; immediately Captain Standish insisted that a fort be built at the top of the hill. The Separatists protested; their own Indian neighbors were friendly! But reluctantly Bradford agreed with Standish; they were outgrowing the common house, and a large, sturdy fort could also be used for Sabbath and civil meetings.

Everyone had to work extra hard hauling logs for the fort, splitting clapboards for the new houses, keeping rabbits, deer, and raccoons out of the struggling crops, and trying to increase their skills in hunting and fishing in order to keep from starving. Everyone, that is, except Weston's men, who used Plymouth Plantation freely as "home base" while they explored the northern coast for a good place to settle but did nothing to help with the work or add to the food supply.

Toward the end of June, another sail appeared on the horizon. "A ship! A ship!" cried the boys with delight. Nothing was more exciting than waiting in suspense for a ship to come close enough to reveal whether it was friend or foe and imagining all the wonderful things a ship might bring from England.

To be safe, the cannons and muskets were loaded. But finally the cry went up, "It's flying the Union Jack!"

The *Discovery* was on its way home to England from Jamestown in Virginia, stopping to trade along the way. It carried no supplies or passengers for Plymouth, but it did bring letters for many of the colonists and news from the Separatist congregation back in Leyden, Holland. The Brewster household was abuzz that night as they shared news and letters.

"Patience writes that she and Fear are definitely planning to join us next spring or summer!" Mistress Brewster cried joyfully, rereading the letter from her daughters. She beamed at Elizabeth. "We named her 'Fear of the Lord,' and she's sixteen now—just a year older than thou art. But, oh, what a head for learning that girl has! We insisted she stay in Holland, where she could find opportunities to study. Patience agreed to stay and look after her—six years older, she is."

Elizabeth nodded politely and ground the dried herbs in her bowl with more force than necessary. A familiar, empty feeling settled in her stomach. Fear and Patience Brewster were coming to live in the Brewster household—two *real* daughters. Why would the Brewsters want her to stay any longer? Even if they did, there wouldn't be enough room. But where else could she go? She didn't want to go wandering from household to household, like a lost puppy. Worse, maybe she'd get moved someplace like the

Billington household! She could almost hear Goody Billington's shrill voice ringing in her ears and the boys mocking, "Good day, Freckle Face." Elizabeth shuddered.

"William," mused Elder Brewster, holding the letter in his hand closer to the firelight. "Pastor Robinson writes that Thomas Southworth has died." He looked up at the younger man. "Did thou not know his wife, Alice, before she was married?"

Bradford nodded slowly. "Yes. I knew Alice Carpenter and her family well." He squirmed awkwardly. "She was—is—a fine woman."

"*And* free to marry again," Brewster said pointedly.

"But surely she has children."

"Who need a father, just as thy son needs a mother."

Everyone in the household stared at Elder Brewster's boldness.

"The *Discovery* could take a return letter," the older man prompted.

Bradford deftly changed the subject. "By the by, young John Alden spoke to me the other day and asked permission to wed Priscilla Mullins."

"Oh marry, I'm glad to hear that!" Mistress Brewster laughed. "I was afraid he'd wait so long, Captain Standish might speak for her first! A nice enough man, that Standish, but he needs a wife closer to his own age."

Elizabeth quickly excused herself and stepped outside the clapboard house into the late twilight of summer. She blinked back a few tears and took a deep breath of the salty air. Crickets sawed away in the forest, and out on the calm bay, lanterns lit up the deck of the *Discovery*.

If the *Discovery* could take a letter back to England, maybe it had room for a passenger. She would not miss her chance this time. She was foolish to think that John Howland might take any notice of her. She had been with him every day while he recovered from his wound, yet he had scarcely spoken to her. Why should he? She and Mary Chilton had looked down on him when he was just a servant. Now he was his own master, and she just an orphan with no property, no dowry—nothing. Maybe he didn't like red hair and freckles!

But she'd have to get permission from Governor Bradford to return to England. She could hardly talk to the man without stuttering. But that was silly. What happened on the *Mayflower* two years ago was fading from everyone's memory. Why, Elder Brewster was even talking about Bradford getting married again! There was no way around it. She'd just have to find the courage to talk to the governor face-to-face.

But finding a time to talk to Governor Bradford alone was like trying to find a time when no bees were home in the hive. During the daytime, he was busy working in his shirt sleeves alongside all the other men building the fort and new houses. And at night, privacy simply didn't exist in the crowded Brewster household.

Unwittingly, Elder Brewster provided the answer. "William," he said one night, "I have talked to thy assistant governor and some of the others, and we are all agreed that one of the new houses should be the governor's house. It is only fitting! How canst thou do thy work here? Thou was elected again at the new year, and overseeing this growing people must be thy first priority. Nay, nay—thy protests are useless. This is one decision that has been made without thee."

Elizabeth was given the task of helping to set up the governor's house. At first she accepted eagerly, thinking surely now she could find a chance to speak to him alone. But when Mistress Brewster marched to the storehouse to dig Bradford's household goods out of storage—whatever had not been traded to the Indians for food or furs—Elizabeth pulled back.

"Whatever is the matter with thee, girl?" Mistress Brewster said. "Be careful with these teacups now, so as not to break them."

Elizabeth felt frozen. She couldn't touch these things! They had belonged to Dorothy Bradford, probably wedding presents. For months she had managed not to even think about the woman or the knowledge she carried about that terrible night. She didn't *want* to be reminded of her.

But how could she refuse to help without explaining herself to Mistress Brewster? Soon . . . soon she would be gone from here and not have to face the past ever again. With that thought to spur her on, Elizabeth managed to unpack Bradford's barrels and sacks, lay out the mugs and trenchers on the rough cedar table, make up the hard wooden bed with the duck feather mattress, and lay a fire in the wide fireplace at one end of the new house.

She was trimming the only candle she could find when William Bradford stopped by to see if his new house was ready. "I thank thee, Elizabeth," he said

kindly, "for readying my new home. I must say, it will feel good to sit by my own fire once again."

Normally, Elizabeth would have nodded dumbly, then made her exit as quickly as possible. But this time she didn't move. "I p-pray thee, may I speak to thee, G-Governor Bradford?" she stammered.

He looked at her curiously. "Of course. Speak."

"I would like thy permission to return to England on the *Discovery* when it sails," she blurted. "I . . . I have no family here and—"

His eyebrows lifted in surprise. "Dost thou have family back in England?" he asked.

She nodded. "Two married sisters."

Bradford's eyebrows came down in a puzzled frown. "Have these sisters invited thee to come live with them, Elizabeth? I mean, are they expecting thee?"

"N-no," she said, startled. "But I'm sure it would be all right."

William Bradford was silent for several minutes. Elizabeth looked at the hard-packed dirt floor. Finally he spoke. "When thy mother and father died, Elizabeth, we—the whole colony—became responsible for thee. How old art thou—fifteen? I could not send thee to England without knowing that someone was expecting thee and ready to give thee a home."

"But—!" she started to protest, but he held up his hand.

"This much I will do. I will write a letter to thy sisters and send it with the captain of the *Discovery*. If they agree to be thy guardian, then thou may return to England with our blessing—Oh, what is it, Squanto?"

Squanto had appeared in the doorway of the new house, looking for the governor. "Much corn is gone from fields ready to harvest—"

"What?!" Bradford exclaimed, jumping to his feet.

"Squanto suspects Weston's men have been stealing corn to trade for furs—though Squanto cannot prove."

Elizabeth watched as the two men hurried out of the house. She followed slowly, walking down the hill to the Brewsters' house. It was not what she wanted, but it was a start. She had made her request; Governor Bradford would write the letter. Now she would have to wait and see.

The second harvest was poor indeed. No one could prove that Weston's men had stolen the corn, and they denied it hotly, but the whole colony sighed in relief when the freeloaders found a place to set up a trading post to the north, called Wessagusset, and swaggered off. Watching them go, William Bradford muttered, "I fear they will make us no friends among the Indian tribes to the north."

With a poor harvest, the colony desperately needed corn and beans to get them through the coming winter, as well as beaver pelts to send back to England to repay their debt to the Merchant Adventurers. With a supply of knives and beads bought from the cargo of the *Discovery*, Governor Bradford, Squanto, Edward Winslow, and a handful of armed men headed south in the shallop to trade with the Indians along the Cape.

While they were gone, Elizabeth busied herself in the woods with Nooma and her children, collecting as many herbs as she could before the frost killed them. Hobomok smoked his pipe peacefully by the fire as his wife and the English girl tied herbs for drying. Watching him out of the corner of her eye, Elizabeth wondered how Governor Bradford had resolved Chief Massasoit's demands for Squanto's life, but a truce must have been declared. Still, there was no love lost between the two Indian residents of Plymouth. Mainly they kept their distance, with Hobomok as Captain Standish's constant companion, just as Squanto placed himself at Governor Bradford's side.

One week, then two weeks went by, and still the trading expedition had not returned. Then one day Governor Bradford and the other men walked into the stockade, looking footsore and hungry. Everyone gathered around, asking questions all at once.

"Fear not, good people," Bradford said, calming them down. "We had good success. But a gale blew the shallop ashore across the bay, and it is damaged. We had to leave twenty-eight barrels of corn and beans buried in the sand. We will retrieve them in good time." He smiled wearily. "It's only a fifty-mile 'walk.'"

"But wasn't Squanto with you?" asked Elder

Brewster. As he spoke, everyone realized Bradford's Indian friend was not with the traders.

Governor Bradford nodded gravely. "Squanto became sick with a fever after guiding us to the tribes most likely to trade with us. He became so ill, we couldn't save him—" The governor's voice got husky. "But before he died, he asked that I pray for him, that he might go be with our God in heaven."

Chapter 11

Caught in a Snare

THE BREWSTER HOUSEHOLD saw less of Governor Bradford now that he had his own house, but when he did drop by to sit beside their fire, he seemed to carry a heavy weight. The death of Squanto was a hard blow, and the winter was lean and food rations had to be cut way back. There was no major sickness, such as that first terrible winter, but faces were thin and coughs lingered. Deacon Fuller and Elizabeth kept busy with their teas and chest rubs.

In February, Captain Standish set out with a search party and recovered both the shallop and the corn and beans that the trading expedition left behind on Cape Cod.

"Aye, this helps relieve the food shortage for the moment," Bradford mused to Elder Brewster one night as the children practiced their letters with pieces of charcoal and wooden "slates" by the firelight. "But this spring will be our third planting season and we are still living hand to mouth. Not a day goes by but I hear a complaint from a hardworking man who is tired of getting the same meager ration for his family as another man who is last to arrive and first to leave the day's task. The women, too, are weary of the common work and want to take care of their own families. People are discouraged. Methinks . . . something new must be done."

Elder Brewster checked each child's letters, then turned back to Bradford. "But our contract with the Merchant Adventurers doesn't allow for personal profits until the debt is paid for our passage. Then all property is to be divided by shares with them after seven years." He cocked a curious eyebrow. "What dost thou propose?"

"I'm thinking we should give each family their own field of corn—one acre per person—and let them eat the results of it."

"And the unmarried men and women?"

"Assign them and their acre to families for the time being, so no one must work alone."

"And our debt to the Merchant Adventurers?"

"We must still work together to repay our debt, whether cutting clapboard or trading corn from our fields for furs. But my hope is there will be more will to work if each is filling his own cupboard with food."

The colonists eagerly received the plan. As spring touched the air, even Elizabeth herded Humility and Henry into the fields to plant their acres with new enthusiasm. Bradford took five of the older orphan boys into his own household to ease the crowding and worked alongside them to plant their allotted acres. When time came for the yearly election of governor, Bradford was reelected by common consent.

After weeks of hard work, the Brewster fields were finally planted, and Elizabeth was released to visit Hobomok and Nooma. As the girl strode past the fields and down the path to Hobomok's family camp with her herb basket, she almost felt a twinge of sadness that she wouldn't be here to reap the harvest from her acre. But surely a ship would sail into the bay now that summer was almost here, bringing a letter from one of her sisters. No, her course was set. She must—

With no warning, Elizabeth felt a jerk around her left ankle and the next instant heard herself scream as she was yanked into the air upside down by a rope tied to a tough, young sapling. Pain shot through her ankle as she hung by one leg two or three feet off the ground. But she hardly noticed the pain as she struggled to keep her apron and petticoats from falling over her head before anyone saw her. "Help!" she screamed. "I'm caught, I'm caught! Help!"

Upside down, she saw someone come running from the nearest field. She couldn't tell who it was because her apron kept falling in front of her face, but soon she

heard running footsteps and a voice cry out, "Hang on, Miss Tilley! I'll cut you down! Just hang on!"

Elizabeth pressed the apron over her face and felt like bursting into tears of embarrassment. It was John Howland's voice.

The next moment, Howland grabbed her and her tangled petticoats around the waist, reached up with his hunting knife, and sliced through the rope that was holding her foot in the air. Carefully he turned her right side up and set her down on the path. "Art thou all right, Miss Tilley?" he asked anxiously.

"Yes, yes, I'm all right!" she choked, trying not to cry. Her coif had fallen off and her hair had tumbled in tangled curls over her face so that she couldn't see. She tried to get to her feet, but a stab of pain from her ankle brought the tears streaming, and she sat down hard on the ground again.

"Thy ankle—it might be broken," John Howland worried. Ignoring her protests he picked her up in his arms and carried her back up the path toward the stockade gate.

Elizabeth had never felt so helpless or embarrassed. She kept her eyes squeezed shut but could hear children come running to see what was the matter. She heard Johnnie Billington laughing in glee. "It worked! It worked! Our hunting snare worked!" he screeched happily.

"If thou art responsible for this, Johnnie Billington, I'll flog thee myself," snarled John Howland, but his long strides did not slow until he had carried Elizabeth into the Brewster house and laid her down.

"Marry! What has happened!" gasped Mistress

Brewster, seeing Elizabeth's streaked, dirty face, tangled hair, and petticoats all askew.

Howland quickly explained and rushed out the door with a wooden bucket to get cold water from Town Brook to soak the ankle. Mistress Brewster shooed all the curious children out of the house and gently unlaced Elizabeth's old leather shoe. A cry of pain escaped Elizabeth's lips as the shoe came off.

John Howland returned with the bucket of water, half of it sloshed over his shoes from running with it, and Mistress Brewster helped Elizabeth sit on the side of the bed and lower her foot into the icy water. " 'Twill help ease the swelling. Easy now."

Howland hovered awkwardly in the room until Mistress Brewster finally said impatiently, "Thou canst go now, Master Howland. Thou has done thy duty. Oh—if thou wants to be helpful, find Deacon Fuller and send him here with one of his plasters."

By now the pain was agonizing, but when Deacon Fuller gently probed her ankle with his fingers, he pronounced it only badly sprained and not broken. "But thou must stay off it for at least a week," he cautioned. "Bind it tightly and keep it high on these pillows."

That evening Humility wiggled herself close to Elizabeth and put her lips to the older girl's ear. "John Howland was blushing like a red sky at sunset," she whispered. "I think he likes you."

Elizabeth didn't know what to think. She was afraid he'd come by to see her, then worried that he wouldn't. When he stopped by the house the next day to see how she was, holding his hat in his hands, she was so tongue-tied she could hardly speak. He simply nodded, blushed, and ducked back out the door.

But each day for a week John Howland came by to ask how she was coming along, and the teasing from Humility and the boys got worse. "John Howland's sweet on Elizabeth!" Henry crowed—but only when no adults were about. Elizabeth reached out to box him on the ear, but he danced gleefully out of the way.

As Elizabeth lay on the trundle bed for long hours with her foot propped up, her thoughts played tug of war. She remembered the feel of Howland's strong arms as he carried her up the path. He truly seemed concerned about her. But did it mean anything—anything special? Or was he just a gentleman at heart when it came to a "lady in distress"?

Elizabeth was soon hobbling about on her sore ankle. She never heard what happened to Johnnie Billington for setting a snare so close to the stockade. But when she limped past him on the way to weeding her acre of corn, he looked away and didn't call her "Freckle Face."

The seedlings popped up in the newly planted fields, and everyone talked about what a wonderful harvest it would be this year. It almost made them forget how hungry they were most of the time. They still had received no supplies from the Merchant Adventurers, and everything was in short supply, from soap to tools. Their clothing was in rags. But hope grew with the green shoots in the fields. If they could only hang on . . .

But as May passed into June, the dirt became dry and crumbly. Day after day, week after week, the skies were blue and cloudless. Town Brook shrank back from its banks. Hobomok said he could not remember a dry spell so long at this time of year. With no rain, the young plants began to wilt and droop. And so did the spirits of the colonists.

When they had had no rain by the second week of July, Elder Brewster called for a day of fasting and prayer. *Fasting?* Elizabeth thought. *That won't be hard. There's hardly any food anyway.* Fish (when they could catch it), lobsters and shellfish (which no one liked), small game from the forest, and an occasional deer barely kept them alive. Most of the corn and beans from the trading expedition had been used as seed.

But everyone climbed the hill to the completed fort to pray. Men and boys sat on one side on backless, wooden benches, and women and small children sat on the other side surrounded by the great oak timbers of the fort. Elizabeth bowed her head and shut her eyes during the lengthy prayers, but for some reason she did not feel impatient. The prayers comforted her. Yes, God had sustained them. God had brought them though trial after trial. They were helpless now. Only God could bring the rain and save their crops—and their lives.

At one point Elizabeth raised her eyes toward the other side of the big room. Her eyes met the eyes of John Howland. Startled, she glanced quickly away.

Had he been looking at her? She wanted to look again to see if he was blushing, but her own face felt hot and flushed.

The day of fasting and prayer continued late into the afternoon. It was hot in the fort, and water was brought from the brook for the whimpering children. But at the end of the day, as the colonists solemnly walked back down the hill toward their houses, Elizabeth felt a cool breeze against her cheek. Glancing upward, she realized the sky was covered with a solid blanket of clouds.

That night, a gentle rain began to fall. It fell off and on for fourteen days, soaking the ground, filling the brook, turning Plymouth's Main Street into a slippery hill of mud. The parched green shoots in the fields straightened and seemed to grow overnight.

"Thank You, Father in Heaven," whispered Elizabeth one evening as she stood in the Brewsters' doorway and let the gentle rain fall on her face. It was the first time she had ever prayed her own prayer.

The day after the rain stopped and the skies cleared, a ship sailed into the bay. To her surprise, Elizabeth's first thought was, *No, no, not yet! I don't know whether I want to go!* She watched the ship grow larger, drop anchor, furl its sails, then lower a longboat into the water.

This was what she'd been waiting for. Surely a

letter would come from her married sisters. Surely they would want her to come back to England, now that their parents were dead. If so, she could return on this very ship. So why did she feel so confused inside?

Because, she admitted to herself, maybe, just maybe John Howland might care for her. But he had not said so. In fact, he had done nothing but show some kindness to her when she had an accident, as any well-meaning gentleman might. Still, the way she caught him looking at her, the way he blushed . . . she needed more time. She had to know!

Many passengers were rowed to shore from the *Anne* in the ship's longboats. Elizabeth watched in delight as Deacon Fuller's wife was helped from the longboat and wrapped in his arms. They had not seen each other in three years. Then she saw Governor Bradford picking his way over the rocky beach to a woman standing with two young boys clinging to her skirts. *Alice Southworth*, Elizabeth thought. She must have accepted the governor's proposal! Bradford took both of her hands in his and they talked quietly for a few minutes. Then he offered her his arm and they began walking toward Plymouth's lower gate. They passed Captain Standish, who moved through the crowd, bowed gallantly to a pleasant-faced woman, and offered her his arm. Myles Standish must have written a letter of proposal, too! Elizabeth grinned.

Elizabeth couldn't help noticing that the passengers from the *Anne* were dressed in clothes that still had a rich color. In comparison, her own clothes were faded, patched, and threadbare.

Just then she heard Mistress Brewster cry, "Fear! Patience! My dear girls!" Two lovely young women were swept into the arms of Elder Brewster and his wife, with Jonathan, Love, and Wrestling not far behind. So the Brewsters' daughters had come at last. Tears sprang to Elizabeth's eyes, but she blinked them away rapidly when a voice spoke behind her.

"Many happy meetings today, I see."

Elizabeth swallowed. "Yes," she said, not looking around, but she knew it was John Howland.

He did not speak further but just stood near her, watching the family reunions. Finally he said, "How is thy ankle now, Miss Tilley?"

"Much better, thank thee," Elizabeth said—and wanted to kick herself when her throat tightened and the words came out in a squeak. She tried to redeem herself. "I never thanked thee for cutting me down on that dreadful day." There. Her voice sounded calm, in control.

"It was nothing. The least I could do for thy kindness in treating my leg wound." Then Howland politely excused himself and went to help carry the baggage of the newcomers up the hill.

Nothing? Elizabeth's spirit sank. What did he mean by "it was nothing"? With a sigh, she walked back to her unfinished tasks.

That evening much laughter filled the Brewster household. The family was reunited at last. Fear was seventeen, just a year older than Elizabeth, but

Elizabeth felt shy of all her "book learning." She tried to set out the supper without calling attention to herself. But suddenly Elder Brewster said, "Oh marry, Elizabeth, I almost forgot! A letter has come from Bedfordshire. Governor Bradford would like to see thee about it tomorrow morning. Mistress Brewster can go with thee."

Chapter 12

The Secret Comes Out

A s Elizabeth and Mistress Brewster walked up the hill to the governor's house the next morning, her thoughts and feelings were churning. Why had the governor asked Mistress Brewster to come, too? Maybe it was bad news from home. Maybe her sisters had fallen ill and died. No, no, that couldn't be. Surely it was a letter saying she could return to England. But now she didn't know if she wanted to go!

"Good day, Mistress Brewster. Good day, Elizabeth," said Governor Bradford, standing politely as they entered the house.

Elizabeth noticed that he seemed to be standing straighter, and a light had returned to his eye in spite of the thinness of his face. Then she noticed the smiling woman sitting in a chair in a corner. She had color in her cheeks and looked sturdy and purposeful. Not at all like the delicate Dorothy.

"Allow me to introduce Mistress Alice Southworth," Bradford said with a smile. "She has done me the honor of accepting my proposal of marriage, and we will be married within the week."

"By God's mercy, Governor, that is good news," beamed Mistress Brewster.

"Sit down, sit down," said the governor. He sat on a bench on one side of the rough oak table, and Elizabeth and Mistress Brewster sat on the other side. Governor Bradford took a letter out of his dark blue doublet. "Canst thou read, Elizabeth?"

She nodded. "Elder Brewster has taught me."

"Good. This letter was addressed to me in reply to the one I wrote to thy sisters. Take thy time and read it."

Elizabeth took the parchment and read each word slowly. Neither of her sisters could read or write, so someone must have written it for them. But the letter expressed sorrow over the death of their parents, and if it pleased the governor of New Plymouth, they would take guardianship of their younger sister, Elizabeth, if he would be so good as to send her back to England on the first ship.

She looked up from the letter. "If this is thy desire, Elizabeth," Bradford said, "I will make arrangements with the captain of the *Anne* to send thee back to England."

If this was her desire . . . "No!" she wanted to say. "It isn't what I want!" But how foolish she would sound. She had *asked* to be sent back to England. She had no good reason to stay, and every good reason to go. She glanced at Mistress Brewster, who gazed at her with a puzzled look. What was the older woman thinking? Probably that this would be the perfect answer to their overcrowded house. That her daughters were here now, and Elizabeth was just in the way. That—

Governor Bradford interrupted her racing thoughts. "Before thou makes up thy mind, Elizabeth," he said gently, "there is something thou should know. Yesterday afternoon, John Howland spoke to me asking for thy hand in marriage and wanted the blessing of the colony. . . ."

Elizabeth's mouth fell open, and she just stared at Governor Bradford. John Howland asked . . . he asked—

The governor was not finished. "I informed young Howland that you had requested to go back to England and that permission had just arrived. Therefore he asked that I speak to thee myself so that thou could make thy own choice about what thou wants to do."

Elizabeth found her voice. "I . . . I would be honored to accept Master Howland's proposal," she said, fearful that everyone in the room could hear the thudding of her heart. "That is, if the governor and my present guardian, Mistress Brewster, think me worthy."

"Worthy!" said Mistress Brewster. "Why, child, thou would have my blessing ten times over. I have come to think of thee as my own daughter, and it pains my heart to think of sending thee back to England."

Elizabeth looked at the gray-haired lady in amazement. But Governor Bradford held up his hand. "Let us not be hasty. This is an important decision, Elizabeth, and thou must think through all its meaning. Thou art just turned sixteen, Mistress Brewster tells me. It is right to be thinking about thy future." The governor paused and stroked his beard absently, then went on. "As thou knows firsthand, life here in the New World is hard, even perilous. Thine own parents have lost their lives. But now thou hast been given a choice; dost thou freely choose this hard life for thyself? Also, thy family came to this New World as Strangers—not of our church. But John Howland is a Separatist of Puritan persuasion. Canst thou embrace with thy whole heart his church?"

Elizabeth was startled. She had not thought about it that way. But her own belief in God and His Son had quietly grown and deepened as she had watched and worshiped these past three years with the Puritan Separatists. Yes, she could embrace their church.

"Mistress Brewster gives you her blessing. I, too, have witnessed thy growth from a child to the threshold of womanhood," said the governor. "Thy work with Deacon Fuller and thy knowledge of herbs has benefited the whole community. But it is my duty to ask thee: Dost thou know of anything standing in the way of marriage with Master Howland? Hast thou been honest and true as a Christian, to the best of thy knowledge?"

Elizabeth suddenly felt as if she couldn't breathe. *"Dost thou know of anything standing in the way of marriage with Master Howland? . . . Hast thou been honest and true as a Christian, to the best of thy knowledge?"*

"Do not make thy decision hastily," the governor said kindly. "Think on it this day, and tell me thy decision on the morrow."

All night long Elizabeth tossed and turned on the trundle bed beside Humility. She could not sleep for excitement and fear. Her deepest desire had come true. Someone wanted her for herself. She would no longer be an orphan, living in someone else's house— not even her sister's. She would have a home where she belonged, a family of her own. And not just anyone wanted her, but John Howland—a young man so respected that his own master had canceled his indentured servanthood and willed him his entire estate. Yet he didn't act proud or spoiled. He seemed to remember his humble beginnings and treated her with dignity. Yes, yes, she would like to be Mistress Howland.

The thought almost made her giggle with excitement. But then Governor Bradford's question came crashing down on her like a great weight: *"Hast thou been honest and true as a Christian, to the best of thy knowledge?"*

No, she had not been honest and true. She had never told anyone about seeing Dorothy Bradford on the deck of the *Mayflower* the night that she disappeared. Had never admitted that she decided not to speak to the woman or encourage her to come back to her bed or even let someone else know that Bradford's wife was out in the wind and cold—because she thought the woman was weak and foolish. Then when Dorothy disappeared and was presumed drowned, it became her horrible secret.

I could have saved the life of Dorothy Bradford.

But she couldn't confess this to the governor. Not William Bradford himself! Why, he was on the verge of getting married again, of ending his loneliness. She could see that he was happy. And if she confessed her deception, he might say she was unworthy of Howland's proposal. Surely it was best not to say anything now. No one need ever know—

Elizabeth sat straight up in bed, breathing heavily, her nightdress damp with sweat. She, Elizabeth Tilley, would know. And God would know. If she was going to marry John Howland, she had to be honest with God. There lay the secret to the peace and happiness the Separatists seemed to have; they followed their God-given consciences. No, she could not look Governor Bradford in the face and say, "Yes,

I have been honest and true," when she had not. It would be a cloud over her own future marriage if she did not tell the truth.

"Oh, Father in Heaven," she whispered in agony. "Help me."

The next morning, Elizabeth walked with Mistress Brewster once more to the governor's house. Her feet dragged like lumps of lead. Again, Alice Southworth was sitting in a chair by an open window, working on a piece of embroidery. She looked up and smiled.

"I hope thou dost not mind if Mistress Southworth joins us," Governor Bradford said. "As my future wife, I feel she may have helpful advice in these 'family matters.'"

Elizabeth just stood by the table as if frozen. She didn't want Mistress Southworth there. How could she talk about Bradford's first wife in front of the woman he was going to marry? But there was nothing to do but open her mouth and tell the truth—before she lost her courage.

"Governor Bradford, I . . . I . . ." Her voice paled to a whisper. "I have not been honest and true and am not worthy to accept John Howland's marriage proposal." Her eyes studied her shoes.

"Go on, Elizabeth," he said gently.

She looked up, and seeing Bradford's kind eyes on her face, she could stand it no longer. "Oh, Governor Bradford, it is my fault that thy wife, Dorothy, drowned!" she blurted and burst into tears.

There was a stunned silence in the room, broken only by Elizabeth's sobs. Then, "Whatever canst thou mean, child?" gasped Mistress Brewster.

And so the whole story tumbled out. Once she started, Elizabeth held nothing back, admitting even her scornful attitude toward the frail, unhappy Dorothy. "Everyone th-thinks no one saw her that night . . . but I d-did," she hiccuped. "I was wrong not to tell, but I was afraid. Because I could have saved her, and I didn't!"

Once again there was silence in the room. Elizabeth didn't dare look at Governor Bradford or Alice Southworth. But finally she heard Bradford sigh heavily and say, "No, thou could not."

Startled, she looked into his face. But he wasn't looking at her. He was looking at Alice Southworth, whose face was full of compassion. "No one could have saved Dorothy," he said sadly. "If you had talked to her that night, she would have ignored you. If you had called someone else to make her come in out of the wind, she would have slipped back to the deck the next night."

Elizabeth stared in shock. What was he saying?

"I tried to make the best decision I knew how by leaving our wee boy behind," Governor Bradford said. "But it was too much for her. The sea voyage was too difficult. She could not face the unknown terror of the life ahead of us in the New World. She became disheartened, and the real and potential hardships affected her mind. Even though everyone assured me the drowning was an accident, I have always thought—though I will never know for sure—that she deliberately let herself fall into the sea. If so, no one could have saved her. Sooner or later, she would have found another way to end her misery."

Alice Southworth reached out and took his hand. He smiled sadly. "I have made my peace with God over Dorothy's suffering. It has helped remind me of my own weaknesses and failures—a humility I need if I am going to govern this colony, where every day is a question of survival. We live each day by God's grace and mercy—not our own wisdom." He turned back to Elizabeth. "As for the secret burden thou has been carrying, Elizabeth, thou must make thy own peace with God and ask His forgiveness for not saying honestly that thou saw Dorothy on the deck that night. But let me assure thee—thou art not responsible for her death."

It took a few moments for Bradford's words to sink in. Governor Bradford did not blame her for the death of his wife! Elizabeth felt as though a great weight had just been lifted off her shoulders. "Oh, I do," she cried, "I do ask God's forgiveness—and thine—for not being honest and true. But . . ." She swallowed. She had to ask. "But . . . dost thou think I am worthy to accept John Howland's proposal?"

"Worthy?" said the governor. "None of us are 'worthy' in that sense. I could well ask that question for myself." His glance fell again on Alice Southworth before returning to Elizabeth. "But our home is with

God, whether here on earth or in heaven. Families are His good gift to us. And our colony can only grow and thrive with solid families at its core. As the governor of Plymouth Plantation, I would be honored to join you in marriage with John Howland."

Elizabeth made a little curtsy and breathed happily. "Thank you, Governor Bradford."

But as she and Mistress Brewster headed for the door, she heard the governor say, "Elizabeth, one more thing." She turned back. "I, too, was left an orphan when I was a young lad," he said. "Then I met Elder Brewster, who became like a father to me and has been ever since. And the church that took me in became like a family to me back in Scrooby, England, then in Leyden, Holland, and now here at New Plymouth in the New World." He smiled at her. "Now that thou hast chosen to stay, I hope that thou canst find thy family here among God's people."

She nodded, her heart so full she could not speak. *Yes,* she thought as she stepped through the door into the July sunshine streaming down on the thatched roofs of Plymouth Plantation. *Yes, I now have a family.*

More About William Bradford

WILLIAM BRADFORD WAS BORN in the spring of 1590 in Austerfield, England. His grandfather was a farmer and raiser of sheep. But the death of both his parents, and later his grandfather, left young William an orphan, raised by two uncles.

In 1606, when William was sixteen, a friend invited him to hear a controversial preacher named Richard Clyfton, who was preaching the "Puritan Principles" of personal holiness and separation of church and state—and it changed young Bradford's life. A Puritan congregation formed in Scrooby, only two miles from Austerfield, and it was there that Bradford met William Brewster, who became his spiritual mentor and the father he never had.

Some Puritans wanted to reform the existing

Church of England from within. The Scrooby Puritans did not believe this was possible and wanted to form a separate church. This threatened the King of England because he was also head of the church, so he began to make life difficult for these "Separatists." When William Brewster was arrested for printing a tract critical of the king for forcing his rule in religious affairs, the Scrooby congregation moved to Holland, where they could experience both political and religious freedom. (England did not have freedom of religion, a representative government, or universal schooling—but these things *did* exist in Holland.)

In Holland, Bradford received an informal education from his mentor, William Brewster, and the nearby university library. He also learned a trade and became a weaver of cloth. At the age of twenty-one, he inherited the small family farm back in Austerfield, which he promptly sold in order to purchase a loom and set himself up in business. In 1613, at the age of twenty-three, he married young Dorothy May, who was sixteen years old. Two years later they had a son whom they named John.

The Puritan Separatists appreciated the freedom they enjoyed in Leyden, Holland, but they didn't want to become Dutch. They were Englishmen and wanted to raise their children with their own heritage and language. The possibility of immigrating to the New World and forming an English colony, but with the freedom to make their own laws and practice their own religion, opened new doors of hope.

They felt like the Children of Israel in exile, and America became their "Promised Land."

They applied for a patent to settle in Virginia and contracted with a group of businessmen known as the Merchant Adventurers to sponsor the new colony in return for furs, fish, and lumber sent back from the New World. Much of what happened in the first three years, including the tragic drowning of Bradford's wife, is described in the story you have just read.

Elected as Plymouth's second governor in 1621, William Bradford tried to resign in 1624, but he was reelected each year. He served as Plymouth's governor from 1621 to 1656, except for five years when he begged off in favor of Thomas Prence and Edward Winslow. He had a reputation for dealing fairly with both colonists and Indians, and lived in peace with Chief Massasoit's people for fifty years. But there were two times during his administration when Plymouth took the offensive against the Indians.

In 1622, Captain Myles Standish attacked a group of Massachusetts Indians who were harrassing another English colony, which was perceived as a threat against Plymouth. In 1637, Plymouth reluctantly joined forces with other colonies in Connecticut and Massachusetts Bay against the Pequot Indians. Seven hundred native men, women, and children were killed.

These events troubled the early Separatists, who had hopes of "Christianizing" the Indians. Unfortunately, the history of New England reveals that colonists killed many more Indians than they converted.

William Bradford took full responsibility for his decision to break the contract with the greedy and profit-hungry Merchant Adventurers, which was driving the colony to the brink of starvation. Eventually the debt was paid in full by Bradford and several other leading officers.

Bradford's own writings give us much of what we know about the early years of Plymouth. In 1630, he began writing his important history, *Of Plimoth Plantation* (original spelling). He personified the vision of the Puritans who came to this country seeking freedom of religion, saying: "A great hope and inward zeal they had of laying some good foundation . . . though they should be but even stepping stones unto others for the performing of so great a work." As for the early settlers of Plymouth, he wrote, they were participants in a "great event, which is the founding of God's community"—but his hope for an ongoing community united in the worship of God was never to be fully realized.

Still, the seeds of democracy were planted by these earnest Pilgrims, especially in the Mayflower Compact, which laid the groundwork for free people making their own laws by common consent.

Three sons were born to William and Alice Bradford at Plymouth, in addition to the sons of their first marriages. Surrounded by his children, grandchildren, and beloved wife Alice, Bradford died in May 1657, after a two-day illness. He was buried on a hill overlooking the colony to which he had given his life in sacrificial service.

Historical note of interest from the authors:

I (Neta) have a special interest in the story of Plymouth Colony. My great-great-great-great-great-great-great-great-great (that's nine "greats"!) grandfather George Morton came to Plymouth in 1623 on the ship *Anne* from Leyden, Holland (presumably from the Leyden congregation of Puritan Separatists). He was married to Juliana Carpenter—the sister of Alice Carpenter Southworth, William Bradford's second wife. (This also makes William Bradford my great [x 10] uncle by marriage.)

George and Juliana Carpenter Morton had a son John, who also had a son named John, who had a son Ebenezer, who had a son Nathaniel, who had a son Ebenezer, who had a daughter Prudence, who had a daughter Caroline, who had a daughter Cornelia ("Nena"), who had a son Ray, who had a daughter Margaret . . . who was my mother.

For Further Reading

Bradford, William. *Of Plymouth Plantation*. Ed., S.E. Morison. New York: Knopf, 1976; Random House, 1981. Plymouth's second Governor's journal of the first years of the colony. (Adult level.)

Bradford, William, and others of the *Mayflower* company. *Homes in the Wilderness: A Pilgrim's Journal of Plymouth Plantation in 1620.* New York: William R. Scott, Inc., 1939. (Originally published in London in 1622 as "A Relation or Journal of the Proceedings of the Plantation settled at

Plymouth in New England," and commonly called "Mourt's Relation.") More modern editions also available.

Harness, Cheryl. *Three Young Pilgrims.* New York: Bradbury Press, 1992. (A retelling of the *Mayflower* journey through the eyes of the Allerton children.)

Jacobs, W.J. *William Bradford of Plymouth Colony.* New York: Franklin Watts, Inc., 1974. (A visual biography. Illustrated with authentic prints, documents, and maps.)

Plimoth Plantation.[1] *"Mayflower II."* Little Compton, R.I.: Fort Church Publishers, Inc., 1993. (Story and pictures of the replica of the original *Mayflower*, which is anchored in Plymouth, Massachusetts.)

Smith, Bradford. *Bradford of Plymouth.* Scranton, Pa.: Haddon Craftsmen, Inc., 1951. (Excellent biography by a descendant of William Bradford. Adult level.)

Waters, Kate. *Samuel Eaton's Day: A Day in the Life of a Pilgrim Boy.* Photographs by Russ Kendall. New York: Scholastic, 1993. (Photographed at Plimoth Plantation.[2])

Waters, Kate. *Sarah Morton's Day: A Day in the Life of a Pilgrim Girl.* Photographs by Russ Kendall. New York: Scholastic, 1989. (Photographed at Plimoth Plantation.[3])

---

[1] "Plimoth" is the original spelling of Plymouth and is used today in the re-creation of "Plimoth Plantation" in Plymouth, Massachusetts.

[2] Same as above.

[3] Same as above.